RAMIFICATIONS

Also by Daniel Saldaña París
TRANSLATED BY CHRISTINA MACSWEENEY

Among Strange Victims

RAMIFICATIONS

Daniel Saldaña París

Translated by Christina MacSweeney

COFFEE HOUSE PRESS

Minneapolis

2020

First English-language edition published 2020
Copyright © 2018 by Daniel Saldaña París
Translation © 2020 by Christina MacSweeney
Cover design by Kyle G. Hunter
Book design by Rachel Holscher
Author photograph © Ángel Valenzuela
Translator photograph courtesy of the translator

First published in Spanish as *El nervio principal* (Mexico City: Sexto Piso, 2018)

Images on the front cover are from iStock.com: antique children's book © ilbusca; camouflage pattern © Laures; tropical leaves © pernsanitfoto; and origami bird © Kuliperko.

Coffee House Press books are available to the trade through our primary distributor, Consortium Book Sales & Distribution, cbsd.com or (800) 283-3572. For personal orders, catalogs, or other information, write to info@coffeehouse press.org.

Coffee House Press is a nonprofit literary publishing house. Support from private foundations, corporate giving programs, government programs, and generous individuals helps make the publication of our books possible. We gratefully acknowledge their support in detail in the back of this book.

LIBRARY OF CONGRESS CATALOGING-IN-PUBLICATION DATA

Names: Saldaña París, Daniel, 1984– author. | MacSweeney, Christina, translator.
Title: Ramifications / Daniel Saldaña París ; translated Christina MacSweeney.
Other titles: Nervio principal. English
Description: First English-language edition. | Minneapolis : Coffee House Press, 2020. | "First published in Spanish as El nervio principal (Mexico City: Sexto Piso, 2018)"—T.p. verso.
Identifiers: LCCN 2020002758 | ISBN 9781566895965 (trade paperback)
Classification: LCC PQ7298.429.A43 N4713 2020 | DDC 863/.7—dc23
LC record available at https://lccn.loc.gov/2020002758

PRINTED IN THE UNITED STATES OF AMERICA

27 26 25 24 23 22 21 20   1 2 3 4 5 6 7 8

For Ana Negri

I too had a summer and I burned myself
on its name

ANTONIO PORCHIA

CONTENTS

RAMIFICATIONS

ONE

TERESA WALKED OUT ONE TUESDAY AROUND MIDDAY. I can't remember exactly which month, but it must have been either the end of July or the beginning of August, because my sister and I were still on vacation. I always hated being left in the care of Mariana, who systematically ignored me for the whole day, barricaded in her bedroom with the music playing at a volume that even to me, a boy of ten, seemed ridiculous. So that Tuesday, I resented it when Mom got up from the table after lunch and announced she was going out. "Look after your brother, Mariana," she said in a flat voice. That was the way she generally spoke, with hardly any intonation, like a computer giving instructions or someone on the autism spectrum. (Even now, when no one else is around, I sometimes imitate her, and it's not beyond the bounds of possibility that writing this is, in some form, an effort to find an echo of that monotone voice in the written word.)

Teresa, my mother, kissed the crown of my head and then turned to Mariana, who received her farewell peck on the cheek without the least show of emotion or any attempt to return the gesture. "When your dad gets home, tell him there's a letter for him on his night table," she said from the door, in the same robotic voice. Then she left, turning the key behind her. She had no luggage besides the large tote bag my father used to make wisecracks about whenever we went somewhere together: "Just what have you got in there? It looks like you're going camping."

When he got back that evening, my father read the letter. Then he sat with us in the living room (my sister was watching music videos while I was trying to make an origami figure) and explained that Mom had gone away. "Camping," I thought.

One Tuesday in July or August 1994, she—my mother, Teresa—went camping.

My interest in origami had begun that same summer, not long before the events just mentioned. At school, during recess, I used to perch on one of the planters and pull leaves off the shrubs. I'd fold each leaf down the middle, hoping to achieve perfect symmetry. Then I'd attempt to extract the petiole and the midrib. (I liked calling the stalk of the leaf the "petiole" and the central axis, from which the veins branch out or ramify, the "midrib"; I had just learned those terms in class and thought that using them made me sound mature and knowledgeable.) I'd remove the midrib and the petiole, put them in the pocket of my pants, and forget all about them. In the afternoon, when I was back home, I'd empty the contents of my pockets and line up the petioles and midribs on my table. Sitting before my booty, I'd take out my sheets of colored paper and my origami manual and, with a patience I no longer have, start folding. I saw my compulsion to fold the leaves of those shrubs as a form of training for origami, a ritual practice I could carry out in secret that would help enhance my manual skills.

But the truth is that I was never much good at origami. For all the effort I put into it, I made no progress at all. Teresa had given me that book with ten basic designs a few weeks before she went camping— before disappearing with her enormous tote bag that Tuesday after lunch. The book included the colored squares of paper, and among the figures it explained how to make were the iconic crane, the frog, and the balloon. In all three cases, my lack of skill was notable. I remember thinking when Teresa handed me the book, wrapped in fluorescent paper, that it was a strange time to give me a present as my birthday was months away and my mother didn't go in for surprises. But I said nothing. I wasn't going to complain about an unseasonable gift.

It would be unfair to lay the blame for my failure on the book: I tried using other origami manuals, and the result was just the same. Even now, twenty-three years afterward, I'm still incapable of making that stupid crane. I was never able to work out the diagrams: for me they were indecipherable riddles, with their dotted lines and curved arrows. I never learned to distinguish when they were referring to the front and when the reverse side of the sheets. Now that I'm an adult who never leaves his bed, I'm tempted to say that I still suffer from that problem and that it permeates my understanding of the world: I always confuse front and reverse. But that metaphor isn't valid, it seems empty of meaning even though it indicates something true. In 1994, everything was charged with meaning, but my confusion of front and reverse was simply the confusion of a boy trying to make origami figures and repeatedly failing in the attempt. And neither can I say that the tenacity I exhibited in continuing to practice origami in the face of constant failure has made me adept in the exercise of patience. What is certain is that origami was a school for being alone: it taught me to spend many hours in silence.

That Tuesday evening, once Mariana and I were in bed, my father went to his room and spent hours talking on the phone. I know because I was awake, unsettled, trying to make sense of an environment that seemed emotionally charged, even if I couldn't say why.

At eight the following morning I emerged from my bedroom to find the house in a state of tense calm.

The three of us—my father, Mariana, and I—had gotten by on our own before, when Teresa visited a cousin in Guadalajara, but on those occasions the transition was always smooth: my mother left us precise instructions for lunch and dinner as well as suggestions for entertainment, aware that my father was a complete waste of space when it came to even the most basic elements of our upbringing. This time, however, there was a lie involved—implying to my sister and I that she would be back soon—and, despite his attempts to disguise it, my father's reaction had been quite violent (his tone of voice on the telephone that first night signaled critical levels of exasperation). And that's why, when I emerged from my room the following morning, I understood that the silence I encountered was just one more of the new experiences that awaited me, changes I'd have to adapt to now that Teresa had gone camping with an enormous tote bag hanging from her shoulder.

I poured cereal into a bowl, added milk, returned to my bedroom, and closed the door. The communal spaces in the house suddenly felt cold, unfamiliar, like those of the hotel in Acapulco where we'd once stayed. With Teresa's departure, the house in Colonia Educación became a hostile territory that my father, my sister, and I avoided at all costs, taking refuge in the sanctuaries of our respective bedrooms. It was in that solitude, littered with failed origami figures, petioles, and midribs without their ramifying veins, that I spent the first part of the morning—of the first morning of orphanhood that now, twenty-three years later, glimmers in my memory like the first morning of history, as if until that point my life had belonged in the realm of myth, and someone had, without warning, expelled me from paradise, making me fall down a rusty chute into the dirty, violent realm of history.

Through the wall separating my sister's room from mine, I could hear the same cassette that had been playing nonstop for the last week: a mixtape that one of her best friends had made for her. All the songs sounded the same to me: frenetic guitar riffs and lyrics screamed in an English for which my classes (where we repeated ridiculously enigmatic phrases like "the cat is under the table") left me unprepared. But that morning, the first morning of history, I understood, or thought I understood, the expressive power of those screams, those clearly furious noises in which Mariana took refuge so as not to hear the suffocating silence of the house.

At around two in the afternoon, my father knocked and, putting his head around my bedroom door, announced that he was going to order pizza. I begged him for a Hawaiian because I knew that, given the exceptional circumstances, he'd give way to almost any of my whims. He agreed to my request with a benevolent nod, and I was pleased, not just because Hawaiian was my favorite pizza but also because my sister hated it. My father was unaware of that; as a rule, he didn't know much about us.

My sister protested. "Mom always orders half and half," she complained angrily, and I thought about my frustrated attempts at origami. However hard I tried, I couldn't manage to fold either the sheets of paper or the leaves of the shrubs exactly down the middle. The middle seemed to be a utopian concept, accessible to the understanding but not applicable to real things. I wondered if it was possible to fold a pizza down the middle, exactly down the middle, and came to the conclusion that it probably wasn't.

I wolfed down two slices of pizza without uttering a word. My father didn't say anything either, or my sister. I thought that the silence would continue until my mother returned, if she ever did, from her camping trip, with her giant tote bag on her shoulder, unseasonable gifts for everyone, and new origami books that would finally reveal to me the elusive secret of symmetry.

That night, after brushing my teeth, I looked at myself in the bathroom mirror over the sink; it was a bit high for me and, as usual, I had to stand on tiptoe to see my whole face. I inspected it carefully. One ear bigger than the other. The septum of my nose angled slightly to the left. An eyetooth had come out crooked—Teresa had warned me that I'd need to have braces fitted, possibly the following year. It would have been impossible to fold my face down the middle, to make a more or less respectable origami figure with it.

I think it was the next day, with the remains of the pizza still lying on the dining room table, when I came up with the idea of stealing the letter that my mother had left. It clearly wasn't, as she'd said when she was going, something that had arrived for my father, but a letter Teresa herself had written by way of an explanation or a farewell. Even for a boy of ten, this was relatively simple inductive reasoning.

Since the beginning of the summer vacation, I'd been reading one of those slightly schematic mystery novels published in the Choose Your Own Adventure series. The books in that collection invited the reader to make decisions at the end of each chapter, choosing between different story lines. The one I was reading at that time was about a boy of my age who had to rescue his best friend from a cave, where he'd been held captive by a mysterious person whose identity had yet to be revealed. It wasn't, of course, the first novel in the series I'd read. I'd already finished another that involved a similar mystery but was set in ancient Egypt, and one that addressed the disturbing possibilities of life in the year 2000: flying cars, extraterrestrial invasions, and so on. They all started with the same caveat that, among other things, said: "The adventures you take are the result of your choice. *You* are responsible because *you* choose." I loved that emphasis on *you*, adored the idea that the book was speaking directly to me, that I was the hero of the story. The structure of those novels varied very little: the front cover announced the number of different endings (as many as thirty) the reader could achieve during the course of the book: some happy, others unhappy, and others just plain crazy.

It occurred to me that, with my mother's sudden disappearance, life was offering me a not dissimilar mystery, one that I could do the detective equivalent of defusing, just as in the Choose Your Own Adventure novels. The logical point of departure was, naturally, to steal the letter my mother had left on my father's night table, lock myself in the bathroom to read it, and then return it to its place without anyone noticing. The main difficulty was finding the right moment to steal the letter. I thought the best idea would be to wait until my father went out to buy something. My sister would stay in her room listening to music, I guessed, and with Dad out of the way, I could open his bedroom door—it creaked—without risk of attracting attention. I could take my time reading Teresa's letter and unraveling the mystery of her disappearance.

More than two decades later, what surprises me about the chain of audacious decisions I took at the age of ten is the fact that I never, not even for an instant, considered the option of asking either my father or my sister what the hell was going on.

While waiting for the ideal moment to steal the letter, I could, in true detective style, develop my hypothesis about my mother's disappearance. "Investigation is using your imagination to follow clues," said the Choose Your Own Adventure book somewhere or other, and that definition felt inspirational, so I gave my imagination free rein in the almost total absence of clues on which to base my deductions.

Maybe my grandfather had died, I thought, and Mom had gone to be with my grandmother. My best friend Guillermo's grandfather had died earlier that year. When he returned to school after the sad event, Guillermo had incredulously described his parents' abnormal behavior: lies, secrets, unexpected departures in the middle of the night.

At the age of ten, I believed that bad things usually happened on Tuesdays. (Now that I'm an adult, I know bad things can happen any day, and even on a daily basis: they are ever present, the fabric that forms the backdrop of exceptional or positive events.) My grandfather might have died that Tuesday. It wasn't a completely harebrained idea. Maybe Teresa was burying him at that very moment. I imagined her digging the grave, her favorite skirt all muddied and her nails black, like mine when I'd been playing in the park. Teresa was always scolding me for kneeling among the bushes, scratching holes with my nails and getting everything dirty. But now that I come to think of it, the problem wasn't so much that I was dirty as that, she said, rats lived in the bushes, and they might bite me. Maybe my mom was burying Grandfather in the park, with her skirt muddied, her nails black, and her fear of rats in suspense until she finished her onerous task.

I took a break from the investigation to consider my progress. Something didn't fit. If my grandfather had died, why had Teresa left a letter for my father? The previous year, when my sister had gotten her finger caught in the car door, Teresa had paged my father before dragging the two of us to the nearest hospital (where the vacant gaze of an elderly woman in a waiting room left me with a profound, almost animal sense of fear that I've never quite shaken off). If my grandfather had died, the usual, the expected thing would have been for Teresa to page my father, as she'd done then, or leave a message with his secretary at the bank. Instead, she'd taken the time to write a letter—a letter I had to read if I wanted to understand the reasons for her departure.

MAYBE I NEED TO START EARLIER. Before 1994, I mean, before that stupid Tuesday. Writing about the past is, as I'm beginning to realize, writing inward, not forward. Rather than continuing the narrative, it makes more sense to focus on detail, clarify the scene while it, in turn, becomes clearer in my memory.

My first memory, my oldest, is this: I'm five years old and am walking, holding her hand. My sister hasn't come with us that day. Teresa and I are walking along the edge of a market, doing the rounds of the stands on the sidewalk: we pass one with themed costumes and piñatas. I stop to look curiously at the brightly colored textiles and she, Teresa, raises the hand that had been holding mine to the back of her neck. Without warning, she falls to the ground. It can't have lasted more than two minutes: the woman serving in the market stand notices and shouts to her husband, in the adjoining stand, for help. Almost immediately, a number of people arrive, offering assistance. But during those interminable moments, before the woman in the market stand notices, I look at my mother lying on the ground, her eyes closed, and think that she's dead. I let out a desperate wail and look at her jeans, which are blurring as my eyes fill with tears. Finally, someone among the people assisting her brings a vial of alcohol and revives her by wafting it under her nose. Teresa, my mother, rubs her hip, which she's hurt in the fall. My wails falter and then dissolve into a sensation of surprise, relief, disbelief. Teresa has been resurrected before my very eyes. She reaches out her hand to me and, still sitting on the ground, dizzy and being attended to by strangers, strokes my hair. It's a miracle, but to me, at that age, miracles still feel natural. Teresa's resurrection seems no more miraculous than, say, the appearance of a tiny plant on the damp cotton wool where my sister had, a few weeks previously, made me hide a seed: the laws of physics don't exist: the world is a more or less painful system of arbitrary events in which Teresa's resurrection outside the stand selling piñatas and costumes on the edge of the market is just one more example. But why is that my first memory and not something else? Maybe because I was then forced to understand that people die, even though they might later come back from the dead and live apparently normal lives for several years.

In the days following Teresa's escape in 1994, I was overcome by a sense of loneliness similar to the one I'd experienced outside the market. At midday on Thursday, my father announced that he was going to buy groceries, having grudgingly accepted that we couldn't survive on pizza deliveries alone. Mariana had gone to her friend Ximena's house early in the day, and my father insisted that I accompany him—he didn't want to leave me by myself—but I explained that I preferred to continue practicing my origami and he let me stay home, with a warning not to open the door to anyone or go into Mariana's room and mess with her things.

As soon as I heard the Tsuru moving away down the street, I made my needlessly stealthy way to the bedroom door with the intention of stealing Teresa's letter. The door opened with its characteristic creak, and I felt my heart pound with every step. But that melodramatic buildup was wasted: the drawer of my father's night table contained nothing more than his passport, a few coins, the key to his office, and his reading glasses, which he never used because he said they made him look idiotic—and there was some truth in those words. Ensuring that I left everything just as I'd found it, I then searched the dresser, the closet, and the night table on the other side of the bed—Teresa's night table—where I found only a few necklaces, an address book, and my last report card (which Teresa had congratulated me on in her monotone voice). The letter was nowhere to be seen.

I consulted my Choose Your Own Adventure book in search of suggestions or ideas on how to proceed with my investigation, but there were insufficient clues. It was like trying to make an origami figure you'd never seen without having the instructions at hand. The letter, the piece of evidence that promised to reveal the secret of the plot, had disappeared. Everything seemed to be disappearing.

Defeated, I waited in my room for my father to return laden with supermarket bags and plastic tubs of precooked food (rice, cutlets, potato rissoles, nopal salad, agua de Jamaica). Since it was just the two of us (Mariana was still at her friend's), my father agreed that we could eat in the living room. We sat by the coffee table—me on the floor, he on the couch—trying not to get stains on the upholstery or the carpet. The TV was showing a rerun of the soccer World Cup semifinal: Sweden versus Brazil. A few weeks before, that tournament had annexed every conversation in the country, as well as my father's undivided attention. I couldn't have cared less about the prowess of Romário and Bebeto, and while this put a considerable distance between my classmates and me, it drew me slightly closer to Teresa, who hated soccer and sports in general. Disillusioned by my reaction, my father sought an ally in Mariana, who took a little more interest in soccer than I was ever capable of.

But on that occasion, sitting at his feet—so close that I could smell his freshly dry-cleaned shirt—eating potato rissoles and watching a match whose result we already knew, I suddenly understood that the situation made my father happy and that it would cost me nothing to feign enthusiasm for a while. This discovery, unexpected evidence of maturity on my part, made me a little sad, as if by taking a condescending attitude toward my father I was seeing him as a simpler, more hollow person: as if, in an instant, I'd understood that my father lacked the intelligence or complexity that Teresa and I—and probably my sister—shared. And so when Romário scored a header in the eightieth minute, putting Brazil in the final (which they later won), I made a calculated comment on the forward's strengths, and saw my father smile innocently before launching into an explanation of the merits of the defender Jorginho, whose "extraordinary pass" had set up the goal. It warmed my heart to hear my father use the very same expression the commentator had employed just a few seconds before. Or maybe I'm feeling that warmth now, and projecting the emotion onto the ten-year-old boy I was then. It's hard to say.

That Thursday I didn't manage to read the letter Teresa had left, but sitting in front of the TV set, I had an inkling of a vital clue to her disappearance, one of the deep-seated reasons that were the cause of—or at least contributed to—her mysterious flight. That clue was nothing other than my father's disarming simplicity, his lack of crease marks (a sheet of virgin origami paper, you might say), the level of awareness—lower than that of the rest of the family—at which he lived his life.

Until that day, my father had always seemed to me one more element of the domestic infrastructure, a sort of robot that provided transport and a certain amount of affection; something between a pet and an electronic gadget. There was no fundamental difference between my father and some of the other people who formed the backdrop of my personal drama—the man who sold newspapers at the nearby kiosk, for example. True, when I was younger, I held him in higher esteem. I believed, as children often do at that age, that my father was a being with incredible magical powers. But at a given moment, that admiration vanished, never to return. Seen from a distance, I guess the change in my attitude coincided with the deterioration of my parents' marriage. Witnessing the increasingly frequent episodes of friction between Teresa and my father, I began, almost instinctively, to take her side. At the same time, my father started to seem like a sullen, irritable man whose unpredictable temper made him dangerous. He, as far as I could tell, felt trapped, and that made him angry and taciturn, wounded by the simmering mutiny of the rest of the family.

In contrast to him, Teresa, and even my sister, were enlightened people, touched by the grace of a god with whom, in my infantile megalomania, I imagined myself to be in close contact. They were Human, dammit; there was absolutely no doubt that they possessed souls. The same could not be said with any certainty of my father.

Now that I come to think of it, in those days I had a very clear organogram of divine influence: god had chosen me to be his favorite human being; on the second rung of the ladder, in descending order of importance, was my mother, then Guillermo—my best friend at school—and after that, without distinction, my sister, one of my cousins, and a few other classmates. Such was my undernourished theology.

As a counterbalance to the deep-rooted Catholicism of my paternal grandparents, my mother brought me up in a belligerent secularism that my father accepted as a given, without asking too many questions (basically because he neither wanted nor knew how to be involved in our upbringing in any meaningful way). Christian precepts were a foreign language to me, and the idea that a man who was born 1994 years before might have been chosen over me to be the messenger of god seemed absurd and unpractical. This delirium of grandeur manifested itself in the most diverse range of fantasies. While I was patiently but ineptly folding sheets of colored origami paper, I'd imagine myself giving master classes on that noble Japanese art to packed auditoriums of enthusiastic disciples. And once, at school, when the teacher told me off in front of the whole class, I mumbled to myself the ritual chastisements reserved for her, certain that god, whoever he or she might be, would do me the favor of administering them in their due time.

My father had no well-defined or even relevant place in the egocentric theocracy of my childhood. He was, for me, some form of peripheral butler, his labors limited to the most banal functions of survival—finding and maintaining a supply of food and putting a roof over our heads—as, I'd been told, is the case of male gorillas in their natural habitat, while the females and their young dedicate themselves to such spiritually elevated activities as playing and delousing each other.

THE FROG IS, IN THEORY, one of the simplest origami figures. It was in the "beginners" section of my book, the second to be explained, coming after only the general advice on how to make the basic folds and the crane. My attempts, however, looked like frogs that have been flattened by a car on a federal highway after a rainy night. (I wasn't aware of that then because I'd never seen a dead frog in such a condition, but life would take on the task of offering me the comparison I now employ.)

On Monday, almost a week after Teresa's disappearance, I made, or tried to make, four frogs with the colored paper that came with my origami manual. Partially frustrated by the results, I read a chapter of my Choose Your Own Adventure book, and later, having had enough of being cooped up indoors, and of the silence in which the last six days of my life—and more importantly my vacation—had passed, I decided to take a walk to the Rec, as we called a section of the park that split Educación in two.

My father nodded his permission distractedly. After Teresa's departure, he'd taken a week's leave, and was spending whole days at his desk (in a corner of the enormous bedroom that he'd designated as his study for want of an independent space) or in the living room, staring at the blank television screen and cracking his knuckles—a habit that annoyed Teresa and Mariana, but that gave me a kind of perverse pleasure: I used to love hearing that thundering of phalanges while we were watching movies as a family.

I put my head around his bedroom door and told him that I was going out to play soccer. It was an unlikely story, one that I invented to capitalize on the complicity that had grown between us while watching the game between Sweden and Brazil, but he didn't display the slightest interest or even congratulate me on my initiative: apparently busy working on some document, he was sitting in front of the black screen and glowing green letters of the computer (our first, bought by my father a few months earlier, which, to his consternation, my sister, Teresa, and I had completely ignored from day one).

The Rec had a basketball hoop (just one) and two rusting goals, around which gathered the most noteworthy local teenagers, who seemed to me like hostile, feral adults whose sole interest was harassing the younger kids. I tended to avoid the Rec; the nearest I got was to pass it when accompanying Teresa to buy the newspaper. On the emotional map I'd drawn of Educación, the Rec was not very far short of Hades: an abominable region where there was nothing for a child like me—with my preference for origami and the shadows, and no love of sports or getting into scraps—to do on a Monday during the vacation.

As I drew closer to the group of adolescents standing around the goal, I spotted Rat: the leader of a gang of hell-raisers, famous for his precocious consumption of illegal substances.

In 1994, my understanding of the word "drug" didn't extend beyond temporary tattoos, the kinds of transfers that came with the wrapping of certain brands of gum. In the Paideia School, which both my sister and I attended, it was said that those gum wrappers were sometimes "adulterated" with drugs, so that when the temporary tattoos (of pirates or dinosaurs) were applied to the skin, children experienced sudden, disturbing fits of madness, and on occasion even died or ended up living in the tunnels of the 2 Line of the metro. That rumor, however over-the-top it might now seem, was for me, at the age of ten, the indisputable Truth, and every time I saw Rat—aware of his reputation—I imagined him in some not-too-distant future, smothered in temporary tattoos of diplodocuses and corsairs, tied down to a hospital bed, blood seeping from his eyeballs. That's why I changed direction as I approached the Rec, before Rat and his cohort of bullyboys decided to relieve their boredom by making me the target of their mockery—as had happened before.

I walked along, folding leaves from the surrounding shrubs in half, following the midribs. In contrast to my usual practice, rather than discarding the two halves of the leaves, I decided to keep them in my pockets with the petioles (one half in the right pocket, the other in the left, so as to preserve on my person the fundamental symmetry demanded by origami). Absorbed in this meticulous activity, I didn't notice that I'd reached the corner of the avenue on which stood the newspaper kiosk Teresa used to visit each and every morning. The sound of the vendor's voice snapped me out of my reverie: "So why hasn't your mom been around lately? Is she on vacation?" I looked at him in stupefaction. That the newspaper vendor should notice Teresa's absence was distressing, and even now, twenty-three years later, I find it difficult to explain why. I considered telling him that Teresa had gone camping, but my voice stuck in my throat, as if I'd swallowed a small balloon and it was there, blocking half my gullet. The newspaper vendor must have noticed that something was wrong, because he refrained from asking any further questions and, instead, solemnly handed me a copy of the paper my mother used to read straight through in the living room while my sister and I were doing our homework, before my father came back from the office. On the front page there was, yet again, a photo of the man in a balaclava with a pipe in his mouth, addressing a huge crowd. "Subcomandante Marcos giving a speech during the opening of the National Democratic Convention," I read in the tiny letters of the caption. There was no way I could have known then, but Teresa was one of those dots of ink on the front page of the newspaper, one head among a multitude of others.

On my way home, newspaper in hand, I decided to make a detour to avoid the Rec, where I guessed Rat's gang would still be loitering, holding spitting contests, whiling away the time until a victim turned up and gave them the chance to swap tedium for cruelty. I progressed along the avenue—the boundary of where I had permission to go on my own, according to Teresa's stipulations—passing a number of taquerías, the local pool hall, and the café where Mariana used to meet her girlfriends to drink cappuccinos and feel grown up. On almost every streetlight, every public telephone, there was at least one election campaign poster: a smiling—and basically menacing—face gazing out at the pedestrians and motorists from the rigid laminate, from its clumsy attempt to seem likeable.

I dropped the newspaper onto the coffee table in the living room and, as was my custom, threw my tennis shoes into the hall. Then I speedily checked out the house to ensure that my father wasn't home. He'd most likely have told Mariana where he was going, charging her with the responsibility of communicating the information to me, but my sister was on the telephone in her room. A few months before they had given in—unfairly, I considered—to her demand to have a phone of her own in there. I sometimes eavesdropped on her conversations with my ear pressed against the door, but this time I didn't bother: I saw a chance to root around in my parents' bedroom again to see if the letter or some fresh, unsuspected clue would breathe new life into my investigation, which was by then going off the boil.

Their bedroom was always in semidarkness, with the thick curtains invariably drawn and Teresa's reading lamp shining dimly. I guess my parents were able to tolerate each other more easily in that light, to hide from each other in the forced intimacy of forty watts, where any expression of terror, discontent, or frustration was dulled or might even be interpreted as erotic.

I remember glancing toward the night table and seeing the porcelain dog my grandmother had given Mom, and which my father had mocked mercilessly for several days after its arrival. It was one of those long-eared hunting dogs, lying in a resting position, looking up with an expression of supreme tenderness. Under the dog, folded and unfolded several times—like my unsuccessful origami frogs—was a sheet of paper on which, even from a distance, I thought I could make out Teresa's elegant handwriting, with its elongated *l*'s and *t*'s that almost overlapped the tails of the *p*'s and *y*'s of the line above. Knees trembling, I approached the sheet of paper and, carefully sliding the porcelain dog aside, read a line at random. "I know there's no use trying to explain why I had to go to Chiapas, because you wouldn't understand." Before I could continue reading, I heard the front door opening, and my father's voice announcing, with feigned joviality, that he'd dropped by the video store for a couple of movies.

4

TERESA WAS, ON THE WHOLE, a serious, earnest woman, with a slightly uneasy smile that barely lifted the corners of her mouth. Her black eyes always seemed to be trying to wrest a secret from the person they observed. She had a thick mane of hair with a streak of gray on the right temple. Despite the fact that my father insisted on buying her dresses and skirts in pastel tones and chic fabrics from Liverpool or Sears, my mother continued to wear the jeans, brightly colored blouses, and huipiles that were the uniform of what she'd been before she met him: a seventies UNAM political sciences student. Her only makeup was a discreet black line on each eyelid (I'm discovering that fact now, looking at photos; my memory, as everything that follows here, depends on secondary sources).

She met my father at a party they both used to refer to in conspiratorial tones that made me feel excluded. I've never known for sure, and even as an adult it embarrasses me to ask, but I'm pretty certain that my mother hadn't planned to become pregnant with Mariana in her final year, and that the pregnancy was the reason why she dropped out of college. The dates fit this hypothesis. My father, who studied economics, must have insisted at the time that a degree in political sciences wasn't going to be much use for anything anyway; even at the age of ten I was well aware of the workings of his unsubtle mind, and that's something he would very probably have thought in the seventies and continued to think to the end of his days, impermeable to any form of change that wasn't for the worse. My theory is that my father was capable of holding contradictory notions: those aspects of Teresa's nature that he found most appealing were also the ones he'd have done everything in his power to modify. He'd fallen in love with an independent, politicized student, but then he wanted to shackle that independence with the yoke of marriage and motherhood. He wanted Teresa to have her own opinions, but only so he could oppose them, brush them aside with a gesture of smug arrogance. He was like an entomologist who becomes enamored with the flight of a butterfly and then decides to stick a pin in its abdomen. I'm shocked to admit it, but I too have loved in that way: almost unconsciously seeking the annihilation of all I desire.

This is pure inference, but it seems to me likely that, with time, the renunciation of her studies weighed heavily on Teresa. It can't have been easy, after the mists of first love had cleared, to discover that my father was more unremarkable than likeable, and that the life of a housewife in Colonia Educación was in fact grim, completely lacking in interest and devoid of any historical sense. If she still read the newspaper from front to back every day; if she continued meeting her university friends from time to time (they told her about their master's degrees, PhDs, and public-sector jobs); if she took part in the rescue efforts that followed the 1985 earthquake, leaving me, a two-year-old at the time, in the care of my grandmother for several days, it was because Teresa was doing her best to resist becoming the conventional housewife my father and society at large expected her to be.

Teresa continued to go to demonstrations during the first years of Mariana's life. My father's reaction to these activities varied. At times he smiled, as if the tenacity of Teresa's political commitment were a loveable trait; at others, he became exasperated and told her to stop wasting her life. She joined committees and went door to door in Educación collecting funds for Nicaragua, El Salvador, and Guatemala. The neighbors were suspicious of her, and the local traders commiserated with my father for, they said, having married such a meddlesome woman. Then Teresa got pregnant with me, and that seemed to calm her a little. A complication in the pregnancy meant she was confined to bed for almost four months, and my father, secretly relieved, hired a woman to prepare meals and collect Mariana from school in the interim.

My arrival in the world involved a—partial—capitulation for Teresa. Since I was a rather sickly child, my mother exchanged support committees for pediatric clinics, demonstrations for sleepless nights. Her work in the brigades after the earthquake of 1985 was, in some way, the swansong of her political fervor, which was then extinguished or went into hibernation for nine long years.

During the months before her disappearance (her flight), Teresa had gotten caught up in ever more bitter disputes with my father. If the violence was contained, the mutual contempt never explicit, it was not unusual for my father to burst into a screaming rage when he couldn't have the last word. From January 1 of that year, with the appearance of the Zapatista National Liberation Army and the signing of the North American Free Trade Agreement, their positions had shifted in radically opposed directions. For my father, who worked in the agricultural and fishing loans section of a national bank, the arrival of NAFTA was an event that could only be equated with the second coming of the Messiah. Teresa, for her part, had her hopes pinned on the indigenous uprising in the Chiapas Highlands.

The residents of the middle-class, conservative neighborhood where we lived seemed to fall in with my father's convictions, and it very soon became apparent that Teresa had no intellectual ally in that homogenous context. I used every means at my disposal to become that ally. I privileged reading over sports, constantly attempted to contradict my father, and feigned an interest in the issues that Teresa thought were important—something very unlikely in a child of ten. And that's why I felt frustrated when, despite my all my efforts, my mother's sympathies always seemed to lie with Mariana. It was to her she turned when she was heaping abuse on the government, as she frequently did. It was as if Teresa's teachings were only directed at my sister—as if she knew I was already a lost cause, condemned to march in the enemy ranks. In recent times, I've shared those memories with Mariana, and she's assured me that I've got it all wrong, that Teresa spoke to both of us, and if her efforts to indoctrinate Mariana were greater, it was because she was older and understood the arguments better. Although it has a ring of truth, this explanation seems lacking: I grew up with the unmistakable sensation of not being the favorite, perhaps because my father's delight at the birth of a son ruined me forever in Teresa's eyes.

Over the years, I've often wondered why Teresa didn't talk to the two of us before she left. Or at least to my sister. For my part, I can now perfectly understand the reasons for her escape bid, and I long ago came to some form of peace with the fact that she'd decided to change her life, leaving me behind like one more element of a world that was no longer enough for her.

5

MY ATTEMPTS AT ORIGAMI GREW WORSE BY THE DAY, or at least that was my impression. Before mastering the crane and the frog, I launched into more complex figures. The result: unrecognizable lumps of paper that had been folded and unfolded too many times. (Paper has that drawback: it's made to remember all our errors, whether it's when writing on it, as I do now, or when folding and unfolding it, as I did then.)

Mariana and I were still on vacation; my father had, however, returned to work. Convinced that it would be best to treat me as an adult, so that I'd become inured to the rigors of real life from an early age, he decided that I could—and should—stay in the house alone. My sister was spending the whole day with her girlfriends, having their ears pierced in Pericoapa or organizing sleepovers that degenerated into parties or improvised concerts.

The prospect of being alone in the house was exciting, but also pretty frightening. I'd heard any number of stories about the Bogeyman: a slightly ambiguous figure who roamed the streets of the neighborhood, putting children in a sort of sack and then slinging it over his shoulder. I didn't quite understand why he would do this or his modus operandi, but as it was unsettling to imagine what he wanted all those stolen children for, the threat seemed real enough to keep me awake at night. On the other hand, being home alone meant having control over the TV, and would also give me the opportunity to rummage in my mother's closet in search of new clues that would help me to understand what she was doing in Chiapas, and when she was thinking of coming back.

When I did find myself alone, the first day my father returned to the bank, I realized that the imperfect silence of the house only increased my fear of the Bogeyman: every creaking door, every drop of water pounding into the sink, the slightest squeaking of the stairs or flickering shadow when a light fitting swayed in the breeze became an ominous presence, a portent of the miserable life awaiting me, being carried through the neighborhood streets in a sack, along with other children who'd been unlucky enough to be left home alone. As I couldn't concentrate on my origami and hadn't yet plucked up the courage to go through my mother's closet in search of new lines of investigation, I decided to spend the morning doing my best to prepare myself for every eventuality: I'd construct a refuge, a bunker that would protect me from the Bogeyman.

My clothes were stored in an unvarnished wood closet of approximately my own height that had a set of drawers on the right-hand side and a rail for clothes hangers on the left. But I used that section—on the left side—mostly for storing board games and odds and ends since, at the age of ten, I had no shirts or suits that needed to be hung up. I emptied the left side of the closet and stuffed the contents any old how under the bed. Then I got inside what could be described as a vertical coffin and sat on the cold wood base with my knees drawn up. It was a good hiding place, or so it seemed to me. There was room enough to spend hours there without having to move, but it wasn't exactly comfortable. I decided that the comfort level could be increased by the addition of a couple of pillows: one for my back and the other as a kind of seat. But as I had no spare pillows, and the secret would be out if I stole one of my sister's or took cushions from the living room, I decided to fabricate my own: I filled two T-shirts with the collection of odd socks from the bottom drawer of the closet. It wasn't a particularly elegant solution, but would do for the moment. I'd work out ways of making improvements to my refuge later.

Finally, with the help of a few shoelaces, I devised a mechanism for closing the closet doors from inside without risk of catching my fingers. When I'd finished all this, I sat inside again with my knees drawn up and shut the "hatch" (as I decided to call the closet door, remembering the submarine imagery that had been the focus of my obsessions a year or two before). The interior of the closet was almost completely dark, with only a sliver of light entering through the upper edge of the hatch. That sliver of light was slightly annoying because, following the thread of my infantile logic, if I could see something on the outside, it was highly likely that I, in turn, could be seen from there, so I spent a while attempting to seal the crack to achieve a totally isolated capsule, dark as night, like the sack in which the Bogeyman carried his captives.

I don't know where I got the idea of calling my refuge the Zero Luminosity Capsule. I guess it was something I'd seen on TV, or read in one of my Choose Your Own Adventure novels, or in a comic book.

Whatever the case, I found a crayon and wrote a small sign indicating the official name of my refuge, then stuck it with scotch tape to the inside of the closet. It was only afterward that I realized what an empty gesture this was, since it was impossible to read the sign in the dark. Notwithstanding, it seemed enough to know that the name of that miraculous machine was written down somewhere: it made the whole affair more formal, added a degree of protocol to the game.

The idea was to spend as much time as possible inside the capsule. If the Bogeyman came looking for me, I'd be hidden in there, protected by the darkness. I rehearsed the drill in case of an emergency—stay still and keep quiet—and it occurred to me that I could put the finishing touch on my strategy by leaving a short note on my bed: a piece of red origami paper, folded and unfolded an infinite number of times, saying, in my spidery handwriting: "Dad gone to play with Rat back soon." This brief message seemed satisfactory, and, after placing it on my bed, I decided that I was ready to confront the fearsome enemy. When the Bogeyman inspected the house, he'd find the note and think that there were no kids around to snatch. And what was more, the implied friendship with Rat would make me a questionable victim: if the Bogeyman knew about the various local gangs (and it was highly likely that he did), he'd be forced to recognize that I belonged to the group of preadolescent hell-raisers who used temporary tattoos with hallucinogenic properties. Such a victim was a less tempting option than some scared-shitless ten-year-old who had been left alone in the house.

At midday I went down to the kitchen and made myself a quesadilla, following the detailed instructions my father had given me on how to light the stove without setting fire to the house. The result didn't meet my expectations. Teresa had never been an exemplary cook, in fact she hated cooking, but she had a magic touch when it came to quesadillas. I wondered what her secret was. Maybe I could go to Chiapas and ask her. My father would come back from work, my sister would return from her party, and they would find the small red note saying that I was with Rat, but in reality I'd be in Chiapas asking Teresa how she made such delicious quesadillas. I amused myself with that fantasy as I ate. I had only a vague idea where Chiapas was, but did know it was a long way off and to the south. I attempted to summon up a visual memory of the map of the republic hanging on my classroom wall, but it was just a hazy blob. In any case, it would undoubtedly take longer to get to Chiapas than to the Zócalo, where my father had taken us one Christmas (in my memory, that metro journey had lasted a whole day, and from then on the Zócalo had become my yardstick for something distant). After the quesadilla I had two bowls of cereal with milk, enjoying the freedom of having no one to supervise my sugar consumption.

I'd never in my life had so many secrets, and that gave me a sort of pleasurable sense of anxiety, like the anticipation before a birthday that, if not kept in check, might end in an episode of bed-wetting. For one thing, I knew where Teresa was (in a place called Chiapas), and then I also had a machine in my bedroom that was capable of making me invisible, my Zero Luminosity Capsule. Those two secrets were dizzyingly exciting. I urgently needed to tell them to someone. If only my friend Guillermo hadn't been out of town; it would have been a relief to share them with him.

Despite my mother's disappearance and my continued lack of success with origami, deep down I felt lucky: I was having the most interesting vacation of my life. I felt as if there were a chasm between myself and my classmates, who would all be in Acapulco or Cuernavaca or some resort, having fun with their conventional families, while I was solving mysterious disappearances, finding ways to avoid criminals, and training myself in the ancient and honorable art of origami—plus the ancient and honorable art of being alone. I thought that when I returned to school, all the other kids in my class would gather around, eager to ask my advice on anything at all, and they would respect the wisdom I'd acquired during the summer. When talking about what I'd done, I might perhaps add a little harmless exaggeration to heighten their awe. I'd tell them, for example, that in addition to staying home without adult supervision for several days, I'd constructed whole origami cities. I could also say that my Zero Luminosity Capsule was really a complicated machine, a sort of paranormal microwave, and not just a closet with cushions made from odd socks.

6

I GUESS MY FATHER MUST HAVE SPOKEN TO SOMEONE (an acquaintance or one of the secretaries in his department) who knew something about bringing up children and told him that it wasn't such a good idea to leave me alone in the house for eight hours a day so soon after Teresa's disappearance from our lives. I find it hard to believe that, without assistance, he would have understood the risks that situation might involve for my mental health. My father was never capable of anticipating extrinsic emotions. The inner lives of others—including his own children—were a strongbox for which he didn't have the combination. He was incapable of empathy, and all his decisions were based on his own feelings and needs. At times, when I think of all the years we spent under his guardianship, I'm still surprised that both Mariana and I have survived.

To cut a long story short, my father decided that it wasn't possible to leave me alone every day, and as he couldn't take me to work either (this would have raised suspicions and generated questions among his colleagues: appearances had to be kept up), he opted for leaving me in the care of my sister. One night, making an enormous effort to break through her absolute refusal to discuss the matter, my father interrupted the movie we were watching (much to the annoyance of Mariana, who immediately complained), and asked us to try to spend more time together "until Teresa's return."

Naturally, "spending more time together" meant Mariana had to be my babysitter and couldn't just take off every morning and return late, as she'd been doing, while I spent the whole day in failed attempts to master origami. My sister looked at Dad incredulously and, with some justification (time brings understanding), complained: "It's not fair. You can't spoil the vacation just because my mom's decided to leave."

Mariana always referred to Teresa as her mom, while I usually just called her Teresa. Mariana or my father would sometimes try to correct me, force me to say "my mom," too, but Teresa never seemed to mind. After all, it was her name. Nevertheless, I now wonder if that difference between my sister and I didn't in some way determine our experiences as offspring. Maybe Mariana was a little more Teresa's daughter, maybe I, as her son, should also have called her Mom right from the start.

My father and Mariana entered into negotiations. In the meanwhile, I feigned complete indifference to their discussion, snacking on successive bowls of cereal with added sugar and trying to imagine endings for the movie that had been left on pause throughout. I don't remember which movie it was but am almost certain it had dinosaurs or alien life forms or alien dinosaurs. Finally, they came to an agreement: Mariana could invite her friends to the house so she wouldn't be bored, and I had to play in my bedroom and "let them have some space."

The following morning, my father left for work very early, and Mariana and I had breakfast alone. She explained that some of her friends would be coming around, and that I was categorically banned from asking them dumb questions. A few hours later, just after noon, the first of Mariana's friends began to arrive: Citlali, Ximena, and Javier. I'd memorized all their names even though they didn't know mine: I was simply "Mariana's brother."

When the second wave of teenagers turned up, my sister's bedroom became too small for them all and they took possession of the living room. They played very loud music and someone appeared with four cans of beer, which they passed around, pretending to like the taste. I made discreet forays into the kitchen for one glass of water after another to check what was going on. It was annoying to miss out on all the noisy fun, but I knew that Mariana would be angry if I spied on them at close quarters. Luckily, her friend Citlali took advantage of one of my trips to talk to me. She asked if I liked beer and laughed without waiting for a reply, possibly amused by my discomfort. "Your brother's really lovely," she said to Mariana, who was stumped by her comment. I guessed that she hadn't planned the beers and was irritated by the thought of having to ask me to keep them a secret from my father. If she did make that request, we'd both know that she would automatically owe me one, and I could make her pay by ordering Hawaiian pizza or talking to Citlali for hours without her being able to complain. But Mariana had no other option: she pulled me aside and made me promise not to say a word to anyone about the beer or the presence of male guests (four or five teenagers wearing huge T-shirts who were attempting to overcome their shyness and talk to the girls). I assumed an offended expression and, conscious that her girlfriends were listening, replied in a loud voice: "I'd never snitch on you." Citlali and Ximena, who were nearby, laughed affectionately; Mariana blushed.

I remember that I liked that feminine warmth, that it seemed a new and desirable possibility: living with Teresa and Mariana, I'd never had occasion to experience it. Both Teresa and my sister expressed their affection obliquely, without falling into the trap of sentimentality or being overly demonstrative. Ximena and Citlali's bubbly warmth was, by contrast, a window into a world of attentions I'd unconsciously longed for since I was small: I wanted to stay in their company, make other pronouncements that would bring fond smiles to their faces, listen to their reedy voices, treasure their gestures of approval. And what's more, I wanted to rub myself up against them like a cat, brushing my shoulders against their knees, and I wanted that odd behavior to seem even more attractive, wanted them to be on the point of exploding with tenderness for me. But that would have been taking things too far: however ominously the threat of being found out might hang over her, when faced with such blatant upstaging, my sister would have pinched me, pulled my hair, locked me in the tiny first-floor bathroom.

As I'd earned the right to join the party, I decided that it would be best not to attract too much attention—however much that idea appealed to me. I stubbornly stuck it out for quite a while, but the truth is that their conversation didn't really interest me. No one mentioned origami, or the Bogeyman, or how to build a Zero Luminosity Capsule inside a closet. And neither did they talk about Choose Your Own Adventure books, even when I timidly attempted to raise the subject. Their only topics were boyfriends, girlfriends, bands, and what they could expect in senior high (which they would start in September). More teenagers arrived—by that time they numbered around twenty—and I thought that there had never before been so many people in the living room; maybe never so many in the whole house, not even when I turned seven and Teresa unexpectedly—it was a first—allowed me to invite all my classmates to break the piñata.

As they entered the living room, the adolescent guests greeted one another with kisses, making me deeply jealous. I wanted Mariana's female friends to treat me as an equal, wanted to feel them slobber on my cheek, wanted them to visit my bedroom to admire just what I could do with a simple square of colored paper: "This is the crane," I'd say. "If you succeed in mastering this figure, you've taken the first steps along the road to mastering your own fears." It was a phrase I'd thought up in case anyone ever asked me about my hobby, but sadly had never had the chance to use.

They ordered pizzas and I ate a few slices, even though there were no Hawaiians: Citlali, whom I considered to be very good looking (her hair smelled of bubblegum), had ordered salami. Shortly afterward, as if attracted by the leftover food or the scent of boredom, Rat appeared. Mariana opened the door and he came in, followed by his band of emulators. One of them had a colorful paliacate tied around his head, like some kind of indigenous Mexican ninja. Another had an eyebrow stud, and that impressed me.

I was surprised to see a local celebrity in our living room. That would never have happened if Teresa had been home, I thought. Mariana's party was becoming increasingly large, serious, and unsafe. I was a little concerned that they might use drugs—temporary tattoos—or have sex: activities about which I knew very little but that were generally associated with teenagers (not adults: they drank tequila and made love, almost direct opposites to taking drugs and having sex, according to my worldview at that time). More beers materialized on the coffee table, and I decided it was time to "give them some space," as my father had said I should. Moreover, my superhuman efforts to be accepted and pretend that I was interested in their criticisms of the ninth-grade physics teacher were becoming wearisome.

I went upstairs to my room and closed the door. On the floor was the note I'd written about going to play with Rat. Suddenly it seemed dumb. I tore it into small pieces and hid them around the bedroom: I didn't want anyone to reconstruct the note, as I'd learned was possible from my Choose Your Own Adventure books.

I attempted to make an origami pagoda. The manual included a couple of explanatory sentences for each figure: "A pagoda is a Chinese house," it said, but no one could have lived in the house I produced: it was a piece of crumpled paper with folds that refused to stay folded. If a family of origami Chinese people had lived in my pagoda, their lives would have been extremely tough. The origami mother would undoubtedly have run away to Chiapas.

7

THE PARTY DYNAMIC WAS REPEATED during the following days with a number of variations. The gatherings weren't always so large, of course, and the pizzas and beer didn't always appear. Sometimes it was just Citlali, Ximena, and my sister sitting on the floor for hours on end, grumbling about their parents' general lack of understanding, making themed mixtapes, or comparing the size of their breasts. But in addition to Citlali and Ximena, Rat frequently turned up, not always accompanied by his henchmen.

One morning, when I left my bedroom after a mammoth session of "blind origami"—a discipline that consisted of folding paper by touch inside my Zero Luminosity Capsule—I found Rat sitting alone on the couch in the living room. I asked very timidly where my sister was and he replied that she'd gone to the store. I returned to my room but was unable to concentrate on anything because I was worrying that Rat might steal the TV set or some other gadget.

As the days went by, I began to understand that Rat's fame was, to say the very least, exaggerated: he was just as bland and apathetic as any other of my sister's teenage friends (with the exception of Citlali, whose scent of bubblegum held me spellbound, returning to my memory in waves even hours after I'd smelled it). At least when he was in our living room, Rat had no temporary tattoos and didn't seem particularly threatening. He did smoke, in an unbroken chain I'd only ever seen equaled by the assistant head of Paideia, an obese woman whose sweaters always reeked of cat piss and full ashtrays. For any kid with a minimum of brains, Rat's ever more frequent appearances in the living room, in my father's absence, would have had an obvious explanation: he was dating my sister. The erotic subtext of the situation was, however, lost on me, caught up as I was in a symbolic reading of the events and, naturally, concerned by Teresa's sudden disappearance, the effects of which seemed to be multiplying by the day.

According to my theory, Rat was there, smoking in the living room, because I'd somehow conjured him up when I wrote that note to my father explaining that I'd gone out to play with him. After I'd invited him into my life from the realm of fiction, Rat had answered my call in real life. The fact that he'd become Mariana's friend was merely a consequence of that invocation.

Entranced by this new variant on my megalomania, I started to spend my time writing false notes on a wide range of topics with the hope that they would have similar consequences in reality. In order to heighten the magical or parapsychological effects of my invocations, I used to pen those notes—expressions of my most secret desires—on pieces of colored origami paper and then fold them into imperfect cranes and abstract pagodas, convinced that this would cause my fantasies to be realized more quickly.

I wrote an alternate ending for the soccer World Cup, wrote about time travel from the comfort of my closet, and, finally, about Teresa's unexpected, joyful return one morning carrying a Hawaiian pizza. But Brazil continued to be the world champions, my Zero Luminosity Capsule was still just an ordinary closet with the addition of pillows, and Teresa didn't return to our lives, with or without pizza, on any morning of that summer. Teresa didn't in fact return on any morning of any season of any year.

8

ONE DAY MY FATHER ANNOUNCED that he'd be later than usual getting back from work. He went into unnecessary detail about the reason for this, speaking of the many implications of the signing of NAFTA. I had no idea then what NAFTA was, but I did know that anything that needed signing was never going to be either fun or interesting. Life had already taught me that lesson. One of the most feared moments of the whole of any year was when Teresa had to sign off on my report card. After her sixteenth birthday, Mariana had spent two weeks practicing what would be her new and definitive signature: her name written in a hand that seemed illegible to me. One day she even practiced that signature on some important document that Teresa had left by the telephone and received a severe reprimand. The previous year, at a school bazaar, I'd had to sign my marriage certificate: my wife—a girl in my class whose name, Karime, seemed mysterious and seductive—teased me about my signature and decided that our marriage was over, only seconds after it had begun. Signatures, in short, belonged to the murkiest areas of the adult world, so I assumed that my father's late return from work that August evening was attributable to some evil force, and I was a little worried.

Mariana, on the other hand, seemed to cheer up when she heard that my father would be delayed; that gave her more leeway in terms of smoking cigarettes with Rat, drinking beer with Citlali, or breaking the unspoken rules of our home in some other way. For my part, I found that need to transgress incomprehensible; not because I had any particular liking for established authority or the rules Teresa imposed on us, but because I loved repetition, patterns, the way the days always divided along the same axis, like a square piece of paper retaining the memory of its previous folds. Transgression, my sister's ultimate aim in life and almost obsessive desire, was for me like folding a piece of paper in the opposite direction to the crease, like ignoring all the clues that seemed to be shouting out for you to choose a given adventure. Since then I've learned that a piece of paper can be folded down the middle only so many times, and that the adventures that lead you to the most satisfactory ending of a story aren't the ones you choose by rationally weighing the significance of the clues, but those undertaken in the heat of the moment—that sheet of paper without folds, that eternal square with no memory.

That day, Rat turned up, as was usual, at about three in the afternoon, accompanied by one of his bodyguards and carrying a paper bag containing cans of beer. He looked cleaner than usual, as if he'd showered before leaving home. I wondered if his escort had waited in the street until he'd completed his ablutions. That's the way it would work. With his friends, Rat behaved like a hardened criminal, although his actual record included, at very most, petty theft from local grocery stores and perhaps the occasional use of soft drugs. His freshly showered appearance humanized him even further in my eyes, as if he'd finally fallen from the Olympian heights of neighborhood legend on which I had set him one day when I saw him from afar in the Rec. If Rat took showers, he probably also had a mom who made him take them. For the moment, I had no mom, so the bottom line was that I could do whatever I wanted, at least until the end of the vacation. That realization suddenly made me feel a little more grown-up—more grown-up than Rat, which was saying something.

Mariana shouted at me to go to my bedroom and close the door. She'd gradually become more confident in her "responsible adult" role and by that time could no longer be intimidated by the threat of snitching: she ordered me around with self-assurance.

Rat ruffled my hair as I passed him on my way to the stairs. "What a crackbrain," he said, and his bodyguard—the boy with the eyebrow stud—responded with an idiotic laugh that didn't sound natural to me. The hair ruffling didn't bother me; there was something companionable in the way Rat treated me, as if he'd been converted into a medium and was channeling the fraternal feelings my sister—a much colder individual—never dared express.

In my bedroom, I tried to read my Choose Your Own Adventure novel but couldn't concentrate and soon set it aside. I discovered that I had a loose tooth. My upper and lower central milk teeth had all already fallen out, but one upper canine and three molars were refusing to go, despite my habit of constantly poking them with my tongue. That loose tooth heralded good things to come: not that I believed in the tooth fairy (my mother had decided to bring us up in a strict form of atheism that excluded Santa Claus and other such chimeras), but whenever one of my teeth fell out, I was taken to a bookstore in Coyoacán to choose something from the stock. Thanks to that ritual, my bedroom shelf had been gradually populated by vampire stories, books with three-dimensional optical illusions or pictures of dinosaurs, and children's novels of every variety. I liked Coyoacán: it seemed a much more cheerful neighborhood than Educación, had books and pigeons and carts selling chicharrones.

Given the imminent loss of a tooth, my dilemma was now whether to ask for a new title in the Choose Your Own Adventure series or the book about samurais I'd seen on my last visit to the store. I thought that the samurai book, being about Japan, might help me develop my skills as an origamist. But I also needed to hone my detective skills if I wanted to work out exactly where in Chiapas Teresa had gone camping and how long she was going to spend there before coming home. Her prolonged absence was beginning to cause me a certain amount of distress, and the image of the Bogeyman dropping me into his bottomless sack, which haunted my dreams each night, with more or less sinister variants, was obviously the result of that distress.

I heard the metal gate to the street closing and deduced that the boy with the eyebrow stud had left. It wasn't unusual for Rat to turn up with someone else, pretending they had planned the visit together, and for that person to then mysteriously disappear, leaving him and Mariana alone. As I've said, all that subterfuge went over my head, although in hindsight it seems perfectly clear proof of Rat's intentions.

As usual, horrible music was issuing from my sister's bedroom, occasionally punctuated by Rat's booming, almost aggressive laughter.

I entered my Zero Luminosity Capsule. The noise was slightly muffled in there, as if coming from a far-off galaxy. It occurred to me that if he was in the mood, the Bogeyman might also steal teenagers; that one of these days he'd come to the house and put Rat and Mariana into his bottomless sack, and they would laugh and pretend to be having a good time (I couldn't believe they were ever actually having a good time). But he'd never find me: I was beyond all that, in an empty, unreachable— really comfortable and radically dark—space where the only things to be seen were the explosions of colors that occur when you shut your eyes tight. I concentrated on those shapes for some time. If I rubbed my eyes with my knuckles, the shapes danced in interesting ways, like the New Year's fireworks display Teresa had made us watch from the roof on a couple occasions.

The minutes, perhaps hours, passed. The explosions of colors on my closed eyelids started to organize themselves into perfect origami pagodas, cranes, frogs, and balloons. Then, little by little, the shapes and characters began to weave themselves into stories. The transition to sleep was smooth, painless. I dreamed of fractal structures: origami figures with midribs folded over like a boy doubled up in the Bogeyman's sack. I dreamed I was doing origami with newspapers from the previous eight months: newspapers with photos of balaclavas and political killings, and Brazilian goals in the soccer World Cup.

Toward the end of my REM sleep, when my body was beginning to feel the effects of being doubled up on the floor of my Zero Luminosity Capsule, I dreamed that I stole the letter Teresa had written telling my father she was in Chiapas, and made it into an incredibly complex origami figure that included various species of animals, multitudes of people crowded together in the middle of the jungle, and a castle with over forty bedrooms, behind whose doors mysterious, narrow, inescapable labyrinths awaited me.

When I woke, sweaty and aching, the house was silent. Mariana's music seemed to have stopped, as had Rat's booming laughter. I remained in the capsule for a few minutes, incapable of moving my legs. I'd spent too long in the same position. I wondered if it was dark or still light outside; if my father had come back from work; if there were any leftovers in the kitchen to alleviate the pangs of hunger I was suddenly conscious of.

I slowly opened the closet door. Once outside, I did the pre-competition warm-up exercises the PE teacher had taught us. I sat on the floor with my legs straight and tried to touch my forehead to my right and then left knee. When I did this with my eyes closed I experienced a fresh outburst of the colored shapes I'd seen just before falling asleep, but this time they were less intense, as if the Zero Luminosity Capsule had amplified their effect, clarity, and complexity.

A languid early evening light was filtering through the curtains of my bedroom window. At that age, I used to find the speed of the evening dizzying. It disturbed me to watch the advance of the shadows, the way they became elongated and crept across the tiled floor of my bedroom like hungry reptiles and then disappeared into the unbounded darkness of night. But that evening was different: it was an evening on pause, as if the enormous floodlights of a sports stadium or spots of a film set were illuminating the street, generating an unreal atmosphere, an exaggeratedly dramatic light, a manufactured dusk. I wondered how long I'd spent in the closet, thought that maybe it wasn't dusk but dawn the next day. That would explain the prevailing calm, the sense of newness that seemed to cloak the world.

I'd never before been completely awake at dawn. Once, when we left home very early to go to Acapulco on vacation, my father carried me, still asleep in my pajamas, to the back seat of the car, and in that drowsy state, I'd had a glimpse of something like this piercing, almost false light that was weighing down on the sheets of colored origami paper scattered haphazardly across the floor.

In the hallway, I noticed that both my sister's and my father's doors were open, and inside each room reigned the same calm and dwindling light: there was no one upstairs.

I rubbed my eyes with the backs of my hands (new, still tenuous shapes exploded behind my eyelids) and went down to the living room to check the clock. I was disoriented; the Zero Luminosity Capsule had functioned all too well on this occasion, isolating me from the world, from noise and the passing of time. Perhaps several years had gone by; perhaps I'd woken in a future world where my father and sister were dead, along with my friend Guillermo and everyone one else I knew.

I mulled over this possibility as I made my cautious way downstairs (the Bogeyman might have been in the house), feeling the cold floor under my bare feet. At the turn in the stairs, by peering stealthily over the bannister rails, I was able to see the living room clock: the hour hand was pointing to seven. Probably seven in the evening: at that time in the morning we'd usually be leaving for school—when it wasn't vacation— and the light never looked anything like what was in my bedroom at that moment. But there was still no way to be sure of what day, month, or year it was. Perhaps Teresa had returned from Chiapas, bringing with her the man with the pipe and balaclava, plus a bag of presents for me. Deep in that improbable fantasy, I jumped the last three steps, suddenly excited.

But the living room was empty. And of course Teresa wasn't there, nor was the man with the pipe and balaclava. Mariana wasn't there either, nor my father. The TV was on but with the volume turned down, and the images on the screen seemed really weird, otherworldly, as if the programming had also been infected by the strange aura floating between things.

As I turned toward the kitchen, a voice shook me from my dreamy lethargy, giving me such a shock that I almost wet my pants: "Where the hell have you been?"

Against all the odds, that voice belonged to Rat, who was stretched out on the couch. I thought it odd that I hadn't spotted him before. Perhaps he had the power of making himself invisible. Perhaps the use of poor-quality temporary tattoos had given him that power, like some kind of abnormal superhero. I didn't reply because I wasn't sure how to address him; it occurred to me that I'd never actually spoken to him before: I'd only ever talked to my sister in his presence, never directly to him. My father had often told me that I should never address older people I didn't know well by their first names, but that didn't quite seem to fit for Rat. I didn't even know his real name. Should I call him Señor Rat? That didn't seem right either. Moreover, he might be under the influence of temporary tattoos. He might even have killed my father and sister while high and locked them in a Zero Luminosity Capsule or in the garage among the boxes where Teresa stored her university books ("We can't have them in the living room," my father had once said. "They gather dust.").

"Mariana asked me to stay here in case you came back. She thought you'd run away and went out to find you before your old man gets back. You killed the party, kid." I had absolutely no idea what Rat was talking about. What party could I have killed when all I'd done was fall asleep in the closet? I looked around carefully for any sign of a party. Had Citlali been there with her reedy voice and smell of bubblegum?

Rat noted my confusion and added a little more information: "Mariana was real worried, she almost burst out crying when we found your room empty. Where the fuck have you been?"

I suddenly understood that Rat was something like my sister's boyfriend, and I felt dumb for not having realized this earlier: all the clues were there, but I'd passed them over. What other truths was I missing? My detective skills had let me down. I was a bad detective, a bad origamist, and even a bad brother. Giant cracks were appearing in my megalomania.

The revelation that Rat was in some way part of my extended family was a shock, but I decided to keep my opinion to myself until Teresa came back: she'd never allow such a relationship. My father, on the other hand, was completely unaware of the sort of person Rat was, and had neither the instinct nor intuition needed to understand that the relationship was bad news, that it presaged my sister's undoing, her addiction to temporary tattoos or membership in a gang of neighborhood lowlifes.

"I was in my Zero Luminosity Capsule," I proudly replied as if challenging him to believe me.

"Hell, you're a crazy kid," he retorted, smiling for the first time.

In the dining room, a slanting light entered through a gap in the window frame. The living room was a little darker. With the exception of my and Mariana's bedrooms, the house never caught the sun.

I asked Rat what day it was; his response was to light up. The whole house smelled of cigarette smoke. Mariana normally opened the windows when she smoked indoors, and then lit a scented candle before my father returned (he probably noticed anyway, but chose to ignore the problem). On this occasion there had been no escape route for the smoke, and the smell was repulsive. Rat was an anxious smoker; he used to take rapid drags on his cigarettes, seemingly feeling that it would be bad luck to let them burn down on their own.

Teresa used to smoke now and again, but always outside the house, leaning against the wall by the garage door; I remember seeing her there when I came home from school, hunched under the weight of my backpack. Teresa smoking with an absent air, giving me a distracted kiss, looking toward the end of the cul-de-sac (a dead-end street, like her marriage, like the whole country, like the obsession with writing everything down that, twenty-three years later, has me bedbound.)

Rat stubbed out his cigarette in an ashtray and went to the kitchen to put the butt in the trash. I was surprised by this action, which displayed a level of care I hadn't thought him capable of. He usually left his butts ground on a plate, and it was my sister or Citlali who collected them up, worried about keeping the house presentable.

In spite of the urgency of the situation (at that very moment, my sister might be finally convinced that the Bogeyman existed and had kidnapped me), Rat was keeping his cool, perhaps—I thought—because at heart he didn't take it seriously, or maybe it was just that the alcohol he'd consumed had affected his tongue.

"I'm going to my room to do origami," I said, in no mood for acting friendly. My sister would get tired of looking for me and return home. I was ready to start toward the stairs, but as soon as I'd turned my back on Rat, he detained me, grasping my shoulder with a firm, heavy hand. "No way, knucklehead. You're coming with me. We're going to look for your sis."

9

WHEN RAT HAD BANGED THE GATE SHUT BEHIND US, I was able to confirm that it was not early morning, as I'd believed for an instant, but evening. That was a shame: going out early in the morning to scour the streets of Educación in the company of the legendary Rat would have heightened the drama when I told my story to Guillermo and everyone else in the class.

At that hour, the street was completely deserted. But then my street was always deserted, at any hour. Groups of children playing soccer in the middle of the cul-de-sac, the goalposts marked by bundles of backpacks and sweatshirts, was a rare sight. But there were no children, backpacks, or sweatshirts there now, the street was empty, or almost empty: in the distance, at the junction with the main avenue, I could just make out the figure of the man from the fruit store closing the metal grille of his premises.

This may sound like exaggeration, but the truth is that, at the age of ten, I was deeply concerned about the subject of consciousness. That's to say, I frequently had that sense of disquiet and estrangement that is the basis of philosophy—but also of all angst—and that causes us to question why we're thinking what we're thinking, why we're alive, why being rather than nothingness, and so on. According to my childish theology, which I've already outlined above, any god directly involved in my upbringing was or should be in charge of all that stuff. But he was sometimes absent or at others seemed slightly less plausible than usual, and then a sense of absurdity, gratuitousness, and imminent disaster closed in on me. True, I didn't then have the words to express all this. I was simply moving through the world with a confidence that would suddenly evaporate, making me feel vulnerable, small, at the mercy of any peril.

That evening, walking beside Rat through the neighborhood streets, I suffered one of those episodes of metaphysical angst: an unfolding of my being (reverse origami) and a profound sense of helplessness. There was no raison d'être underlying anything. However many letters I stole, I'd never know the real reason for Teresa's departure. However many

Zero Luminosity Capsules I constructed, and however many hours I spent inside them, I'd never succeed in disappearing completely or making myself invisible to the agents of evil. And however many leaves and sheets of paper I folded down the middle, origami wasn't going to give meaning to anything at all, because symmetry wasn't a material state but an invention of the mind; half a sheet of paper was always imperfect and, therefore, the cranes, frogs, pagodas, and kimonos made of folded paper had a lie at their very cores, as do, of course, flesh-and-blood humans: we, too, are formed from a fundamental lie, or at least a fiction (a redemptive lie). If the fold that is the basis of origami rests on a false premise, the same can be said of the innermost fold of our personalities, the fold no one can ever access, the fold of our selves—the dolorous reverse side we hide, conceal like a secret letter in the night table of life; that fold, I'd tell myself, is also an optical illusion, and in fact our only essence is our fears, our only identity our frustrations, our only meaning our cry in the deep shadows of time.

Naturally, I didn't think all that at the age of ten, I'm projecting these reflections onto the inexpressible concern I experienced then as a sort of bubble stuck at some indefinite point within my sickly rib cage.

It isn't always easy for me to make that distinction, to know for sure if my memories are simply a projection of what—lying here on the left side of a double bed, surrounded by packets of pills and notebooks full of crossings-out—I think now, twenty-three years later. Memories are fabrications that bear little relationship to their supposed origins, and each and every time we recall something, that memory becomes more autonomous, more detached from the past, as if the cord holding it to life itself is fraying until one day, it snaps and the memory bolts, runs free through the fallow field of the spirit, like a liberated goat taking to the hills.

Rat took a pack of cigarettes from the pocket of his denim jacket and offered me one. To be polite, I took it. He then moved the flickering flame of his lighter close to my face, and I took a deep suck. I coughed, the flame went out, and at the exact instant when it disappeared, it occurred to me that Teresa might be dead. It was a fleeting thought, one I hadn't had since the time my mother fainted on the edge of the market, by the stand selling piñatas and themed costumes. And although that idea darkened my mood like a cloud suddenly casting a shadow over everything, I didn't share my thoughts.

Rat lit his own cigarette and took a long drag, expelling the smoke simultaneously through his nostrils and mouth, while I made careful note of the process, eager to learn how to smoke like my improbable hero.

The streets of Educación were, and still are, identical: cul-de-sacs branching out from a secondary avenue that leads to a wider one. There was the Rec, with its rusty goal and, in another small park behind an elementary school, a couple of slides—also rusty.

Originally constructed to house workers affiliated with the union of state-owned oil company employees, the neighborhood later became the territory of the teaching equivalent, which immediately wanted to put its own stamp on it: the streets are all indicated by letters and the avenues by numbers. Some of the main avenues bear the names of union bosses, as if the alphabet included their heroic deeds.

In Educación, it was always necessary to refer to the block you were talking about, because two streets might have the same name. The blocks, for their part, were shown in Roman numerals. By the age of six, I'd memorized my address (No. 23, Calle H, Block III, off Avenida 2) at the insistence of Teresa, who invented a jingle to make it easier to remember and repeat that uninspiring alphanumerical sequence. My friend Guillermo was very surprised that places in my neighborhood sounded like moves in a game of Battleship, where you sink enemy ships by giving their location using the Cartesian coordinate system. He used to say that it was like I'd learned the coordinates of my house instead of my address. I hadn't the faintest idea what coordinates were but, too ashamed to ask, would just give a forced laugh.

The cigarette that Rat offered me and the episode of metaphysical angst joined forces to leave me suddenly dizzy; I experienced a sort of feverishness, with a simultaneous sense of clarity that perhaps derived from nausea. I thought I was going to throw up, but luckily nothing emerged from my mouth. Rat glanced in my direction and laughed quietly. He gave me a friendly punch on the back, which didn't hurt and made me feel grown up, his equal. Could it be that Rat was now my friend? Then he plucked the cigarette from my mouth and took a drag on it while still smoking his own. The two cigarettes hung from his lower lip as if by magic, kept there by some unknowable force. He took them from his mouth with his right hand and exhaled the smoke, a lot of smoke, through his nostrils and mouth, just as he'd done before. I watched him in stupefaction, unable to understand why anyone would want to smoke two cigarettes at the same time. As if reading my mind, he murmured, "Waste not, want not. You wouldn't have been able to manage the whole thing." I was annoyed by that insinuation, but had to accept—and concede through my silence—that he was right.

We walked along Avenida 3, passing the arcade and Los Orgullosos, inside which rotated the reddish meat of the tacos al pastor. The smell of scorched meat mingled with the less pleasant odor rising from the sewage system. I didn't ask Rat where we were going because just following him was exciting, and, in any case, the whole scene had a dream-like quality that held me in suspense, as if I were expecting to wake at any moment.

We reached Canal de Miramontes, which for me was the midrib of the cosmos, from which branched out the other half of the planet: the part that wasn't Colonia Educación, and within the confines of which my imagination grouped such diverse places as Taxqueña, Cuernavaca, Chiapas, and the United States. All those unfathomable destinations had to be a thousand or ten thousand times the size of Educación, according to my hasty calculations. That's to say, a space so large you could be lost in it forever: an inferno deeper than the sack into which the Bogeyman dropped stolen children.

Rat was chain-smoking as if he found Earth's atmosphere toxic and only tobacco fumes were keeping him alive. (And the truth is, he wasn't the only one to find the atmosphere at that time and place highly toxic: with air pollution levels at about 200 on the Metropolitan Index of Air Quality, during the summer of 1994, breathing was an extreme sport.) He smoked every cigarette right down to the end, until the smell of the burning filter reminded him that it was time to light the next. His voice was nasal and, being on the point of breaking, fluctuated between the deep baritone it would become a few months later and the squeakiness of childhood. Maybe that's why he rarely said much. He glanced at me suspiciously, as if he had something important to say but was thinking the better of it even before opening his mouth. When we got to the corner of Taxqueña and Miramontes, Rat seemed to hesitate for a fraction of a second. He threw down his cigarette, this time only half-smoked, turned to face me, and, putting his hands on my shoulders as if to prevent me from being distracted by the chaos of vehicles and ambulant street sellers, asked: "Do you know where the fuck your mom is, child?"

I was finally able to show Rat that I wasn't a child, that I knew what was going on, knew even more than Mariana. "Yes," I said, sure of myself for the first time that night. "She's in Chiapas. She's gone camping."

Rat's face was transformed. He clearly hadn't expected that reply. Just as his voice sometimes betrayed his former age, his astonished expression brought back the face he must have had years before—before the beer, cigarettes, and temporary tattoos. He attempted to recompose his degenerate-maudit teenage features and scrutinized me as if trying to work out whether I was conscious of the implications of my reply.

"I want something to eat," I said in an attempt to change the subject, but also because the pangs of hunger had suddenly returned. "I fell asleep in the capsule and haven't had anything all day." The peseros and trolleybuses were forming a solid wall along Avenida Taxqueña. Rat went to a street cart, leaving me a few steps behind, and bought a can of Coca-Cola and some Japanese cracker nuts. The woman pushing the cart had no change for the two-hundred new-peso bill that Rat proffered her, and he had to rummage in his pockets for coins. He handed me the plastic bag containing the booty: "Here you go, crackbrain."

I was beginning to weary of his offhand manner, but the adventure of going beyond the bounds of my neighborhood in the company of someone more popular than any of my friends made me swallow my pride: there was something bigger at stake.

Rat beckoned me to follow him and hurled himself between the trolleybuses and peseros without waiting for the traffic signals to change. I thought we were going to die, but followed him anyway, because the idea of being left alone on Avenida Taxqueña was even more frightening. We crossed the street to the sound of polyphonic horns, dodging weary pedestrians laden with packages and suitcases, and arrived on the outskirts of the Terminal Central de Autobuses del Sur. In front of it, the Taxqueña market engulfed the pesero stop and the entrance to the metro, stretching out like an ocean of junk.

A woman passed near me carrying a live, flapping hen by its bound feet. For a moment I watched two children in rags playing a game that involved throwing stones at a bottle.

Just before we reached the terminal, Rat once again seemed to hesitate momentarily. "I've got a hunch Mariana might be here, inside. She knows where your old lady is too." He stressed the last sentence, as if demonstrating that he'd been aware of just what was going on before I told him.

Something didn't quite add up: if my sister was looking for me, why would she go to the bus terminal? I'd never expressed any interest in traveling anywhere by bus. I sometimes used to talk about flying in a jet plane, or even sailing on a ship, which to me seemed exciting and strange, but buses were, in my opinion, ordinary and unattractive. Teresa, Mariana, and I had once gone to Tepoztlán on a bus that had departed from that very terminal, and the stink of vomit seeping from the restroom had made me feel sick ten minutes into the journey. If Mariana knew anything at all, she'd be looking for me at the Rec, or on the slides, or any other place in Educación, but not in the bus terminal by the Taxqueña metro station.

Rat worked out that something was bothering me. I suppose it was obvious (when I'm worried I frown deeply, even nowadays). He spoke quickly, nervously; for the first time I understood that he didn't know exactly what we were doing either: "Look, crackbrain, Mariana was a bit canned. Don't tell anyone. We'd been drinking in her room. When we couldn't find you anywhere in the house, she started crying, thought something had happened to you. Then she began babbling on about your old lady, said she was in Chiapas and something about going to look for her. I wasn't really listening. I thought she was afraid of getting a bawling out. She told me to stay and wait for you and ran out of the house. But she's been gone for around two hours now." Rat paused, allowing me to take all that in before continuing, "Do you understand that there's a war in Chiapas? Tanks and soldiers. We have to find Mariana."

It wasn't easy to digest all that information. That Teresa, a woman with a monotone voice and firm convictions, should have gone to Chiapas was one thing, but that my drunken sister should decide to follow her was much more serious.

Of course, I already knew that there was a war in Chiapas, I'd seen it on TV. For months it had been the only thing anyone anywhere talked about. At school, we'd been assembled in the auditorium, and it was explained that nothing was going to happen in the capital, but Guillermo's elder brother had told him that the Zapatistas were going to kill the president and take away rich people's houses. Even though Guillermo's brother wasn't generally a reliable source of information, my friend and I had gotten steamed up by just the idea of all that. Teresa was constantly muttering insults about the president ("that bald murderer," she used to call him), and at the beginning of the year the promise of his overthrow had excited me for a few weeks. Then, in March, someone had shot Colosio, the PRI presidential candidate—in Teresa's view, he was just as bad as "that bald murderer." The shooting had taken place in Tijuana, which, as we were told in geography class—geography wasn't my strongest subject—was more or less on the other side of the country. That was when the war and generalized fraying of nerves took up permanent residence in the house in Educación. The arguments between Teresa and my father about the situation in Chiapas and the forthcoming elections grew in intensity and volume. Only the soccer World Cup had managed to calm things for thirty days, distracting my father from current affairs.

The clamor of war and politics was amplified at school. During recess, the children in sixth grade sometimes made a game of frightening us, saying that they had seen Zapatistas or—even worse—soldiers behind the co-op, in the vacant lot that the principal had promised to transform into a small soccer field at some point in the future.

One day, a boy in my class turned up wearing a red balaclava with a pompom on top, and fights were organized between the two most aggressive pupils, one representing the insurgents in balaclavas and the other the forces of law and order—who were booed by the naturally rebellious children, the ones who were always talking in class. Later that afternoon, when I told Teresa about those small-scale reproductions of the political tension in the country, she attempted to explain something about the indigenous peoples. Before she could finish, my father interrupted to drag me off to watch a soccer game in which the Mexican team was playing. On another occasion, he commented over breakfast that Chiapas was a beehive. I didn't understand the metaphor then, but the idea of a gigantic beehive containing whole cities and enormous bees gave me a nightmare.

All those scenes (the scraps at school, the noisy domestic arguments, the red balaclava with a pompom, the mutant bees) came back to flood my mind when I heard Rat mention the war, the tanks, the possibility that Mariana had followed in Teresa's footsteps and run away to Chiapas.

I felt betrayed. It hurt me that, knowing where Teresa was, my sister hadn't sat down and talked to me, explained what was going on in our family. In fact, she'd left me to investigate on my own, to steal letters and spend whole days inside a dark closet when we could have been coming up with a plan—a sibling plan to get our mother back—or running away together. It felt unfair that Mariana had gone, leaving me alone with my father, abandoning me to a life of boredom while she was having an adventure.

Now Rat was trying to drag me into the bus terminal, or the war, to save my sister and maybe even my mother. It wasn't particularly clear why he needed me as his shield carrier, but at that moment I had no intention of asking questions. It was that, or go back home to watch reruns of the soccer World Cup with my father, eat Hawaiian pizza, and make non-figurative origami figures until the end of the summer vacation.

Although I was eager to start, I was also sorry not to have come better prepared. If I'd known that we were setting out on an expedition of that caliber, I'd have brought my jacket with secret pockets, and my Choose Your Own Adventure book to act as a sort of guide. But I understood that at certain critical moments life offers the opportunity to really choose our own adventures and decided that following Rat to war would make me the envy of every boy in my class; if, that is, I managed to stay alive until the new school year.

By the time Rat and I had passed through the doors of the Autobuses del Sur terminal, the only outcome to that adventure my imagination was capable of coming up with was personal triumph. I heard a bubblegum-scented Citlali laughing and saw Ximena doling out over-the-top gestures of affection while I told them how I'd found their best friend, my sister, who by then was allowing me to choose whatever pizza I wanted, and was asking—as if she really cared—how the Zero Luminosity Capsule worked. I saw my grateful father comparing me to Bebeto or Romário. I saw, more clearly than anything else, Teresa smoking in silence by the door, secretly proud of her son.

10

RAT INQUIRED ABOUT MARIANA at a number of counters in the terminal. He inquired timidly, as if defeated in advance. Not having a photograph, he attempted on each occasion to describe my sister, but his linguistic tools were, to say the least, limited: he'd simply say that she was a girl with black hair, wearing a checked shirt knotted at the waist. One of the assistants from the line that serviced Ixtapa said a girl of that description had bought a ticket for a bus leaving at 8 p.m., but we checked the waiting room and didn't see Mariana there. What's more, Ixtapa seemed an unlikely destination. No bus to Chiapas had departed in the previous two hours and none was scheduled to leave around that time, but the logical thing would have been to take a bus to Puebla, Veracruz, or Oaxaca and then another to San Cristóbal de las Casas. At least those were Rat's muttered conjectures as we walked from one end of the bus terminal to the other—with me a few steps behind him, trying to look calm. All those names of states and cities sounded vaguely familiar from my textbooks, but I was incapable of visualizing them in any way. They were just that: empty, interchangeable names. Magical names that invoked unknown lands where my mother and my sister were fighting for a fairer world.

Finally, Rat tired of making inquiries, and we sat in waiting room No. 2, next to a stand selling backpacks that also had plush toys and ham and cheese sandwiches. The seat Rat took was falling apart; mine had a basic penis design drawn in indelible ink. The whole terminal smelled strange, a mixture of burnt food and gas.

Rat seemed undecided, as if his vaguely ambitious plan to rescue Mariana from who knows what danger had balked at the first hurdle (what's more, a predictable hurdle, since it was unlikely that we would have found my sister just sitting waiting for us in the Taxqueña terminal). Perhaps he'd expected the first person he asked to tell him which bus she'd boarded so we could get on the next one going to the same place, or intercept it in a cab before it left the city. The idea of the two of us taking a bus somewhere, without any clear indication of my sister's whereabouts, must have suddenly seemed less enticing. Like a fly, his eyes rested on one object after another. I asked if he'd given up on going to Chiapas, if he'd given up on searching for Mariana, given up on helping me. I asked a torrent of questions, but Rat responded with only an evasive gesture that seemed to say, "stop bugging me."

That indecisiveness was another disappointment. Not only did Rat take a shower before leaving home, meekly obeying his mother, but he also shrank before the slightest danger. His fame as a rebellious teenager once again appeared unjustified. I thought about snitching on him to the gorillas who were normally to be seen hanging around him at the Rec, explaining that their idol was nothing but a scared kid with a breaking voice who pretended to possess levels of maturity, and even evil, he'd never attain.

I spotted a terrifying trend: according to all the available evidence, my mother and sister had been capable of pitching themselves into the battle without giving it a second thought, guided by their convictions or by passions that raised them onto the untamed flanks of History. On the other hand, my father and Rat, different but complementary models of masculinity—the omniscient provider, the hardline rebel— remained on the margins of events, watching reruns of soccer games or applying temporary tattoos like self-obsessed loudmouths. What that pattern held in store for my own life was frightening: the world was a place infested with cowardly men who spilled beer down their clean shirts, and the women who put up with them for a time. At that instant, it occurred to me that if I wanted to do something worthwhile with my time on earth, I should, at least symbolically, become the woman whom destiny or genetics had prevented me from being at the moment of conception. If not, I'd be condemned to repeating the mistakes of my father and Rat, to crying over games lost in overtime or hanging around on the neighborhood streets, my hair freshly washed, accompanied by my minions, without the courage to do anything by myself.

Head bent, sitting in waiting room No. 2 of the Taxqueña bus terminal, Rat was inspecting the laces of his sneakers, the dirt under his fingernails, the wide legs of his grubby, torn jeans. His mouth seemed larger, as if gravity were dragging his lips downward, giving him an expression of childlike concentration.

I don't know where I found the confidence and willpower to do it, but I was suddenly on my feet, facing Rat, telling him that we had to take a bus to Chiapas, that we had to follow Mariana and my mother to the war itself if necessary. The words issued from my mouth of their own volition, my voice was charged with emotion. Rat looked at me uncertainly and mumbled something I didn't catch. Then he said that he wanted to see my sister, too, but that it was a bad idea, that she probably hadn't gone to Chiapas, that she'd return home on her own when the drink had worn off and she realized that she was in trouble. I glared at him. The scorn I felt took the form of a tangled knot of emotions that threatened to become tears. I thought that if I went on looking him in the eyes, I'd end up hitting him, even while I was aware he could easily overpower me.

When he understood that I was willing to do whatever it took to find my sister, Rat went back on the attack with new arguments and a tougher tone. He told me that we had no damned idea where Mariana was; she could have taken a bus to Chiapas or a pesero to Ciudad Satélite, there was no way of knowing. I'd never been to Ciudad Satélite, but it sounded like somewhere in another part of the galaxy, and I was surprised you could take a pesero there. I sat down again on the rickety seat, next to Rat. Our options were running out. The clock at the far end of the waiting room showed 8:40 in the evening. I thought that if my father hadn't already arrived back from work, he soon would. A homeless man stopped in front of us and asked for money; Rat ignored him, and I made a gesture indicating we had nothing to give. When he left, I burst into tears.

There's another very early memory I return to every so often. It must have been after the time Teresa fainted by the piñata and costume stand in the market. The three of us were walking across a cobbled square. With hindsight, I've come to the conclusion that it must have been the main square of Coyoacán, but there's really no way of knowing. My mother had bought us each an ice cream, but I'd thrown half of mine to the ground, and Mariana was teasing me by licking hers with exaggerated pleasure. By the pavilion in the square, fifteen or twenty gray pigeons were moving about, pecking at crumbs of bread and fluffing out their breast feathers. Partly as a distraction from Mariana's vexatious behavior, I let go of Teresa's hand and ran toward the pigeons.

It's a game as old as the concept of the city, one played by every child who has ever crossed a public square anywhere: attempting to kick the pigeons and then watching them fly away. One of the attractions of that game for a miniature human is, I guess, the sense of being dangerous: the power wielded over those who are weaker than us—which at that age is only birds. I used to like feeling the fluttering of wings around me, the frenetic flight that left me excited and triumphal in the middle of a cloud of dirty, flea-infested feathers.

On this occasion, however, something was different. One particular pigeon, plumper and less agile than the rest, was my chosen target. Before starting my dash, I contemplated it for a moment. It looked as stupid as any other pigeon but moved more slowly than its companions, as if its instincts were atrophied or dormant. I ran toward it as fast as my short legs would carry me. The other pigeons rose up in flight as I passed; I heard the beating of their wings and sensed the movement of their shadows on the ground. But the plump pigeon stayed exactly where it was, indifferent to its fate.

When I was halfway there, the pigeon showed signs of taking off, but didn't quite make it. There was, in that aborted attempt, a yearning for the sky, common to so many bipeds, but also a real-life inability to fulfill it.

The impact of my foot fell on one of its sides, just below the wing. If I hadn't been a rather scrawny five-year-old, I'd probably have killed the pigeon, but it just rolled over like a rag doll, making two or three turns on its unstable axis. Then it got to its feet again.

I'd done it. I'd kicked the fattest pigeon in the square, thus fulfilling the secret ambition of every child my age who was in the habit of chasing dumb birds. The desire to exercise cruelty had been unexpectedly satisfied. I'd managed to kick the pigeon but, paradoxically, something had broken inside me. That kick had hurt me too.

When I turned to my mother and sister, some fifteen or twenty yards behind me, looking on in stunned amazement, I understood just what I'd done, the gravity of my transgression. And I began to cry.

What I remember most clearly about that whole episode is Teresa's coldness: she refused to comfort me when I reached her, my face smeared with tears and snot. "Let's go," she said, and the three of us walked back to the car without saying another word.

Sitting next to Rat in waiting room No. 2 of the Terminal Central de Autobuses del Sur, crying, I remembered the sensation of that kick to the pigeon's soft flank, near the pavilion in the cobbled square. And although the memory made my tears even more bitter, they also became more adult, tears that—for the first time—weren't the result of a specific, immediate situation, but of the vague consciousness of having lost something I could never again recover.

Rat got to his feet. It was as if my sobs were the last straw, as if he had no idea how to deal with a public expression of emotion. There was fear in his eyes: fear of being judged by others, but also the fear that my tears would trigger something inside him he'd held in check throughout his whole life: fear of crying with me, for me, beside me, like two lost children in a bus terminal.

Rat hurriedly took a wad of crumpled bills from his pocket and held them out to me unceremoniously. "You go," he mumbled, and walked quickly away toward the noise of the traffic on Avenida Taxqueña without looking back.

TWO

1

THE BED IN WHICH I'M WRITING IS DISGUSTING. The sheets are stained with layer upon layer of dried sweat—the geological strata of my sedentary life. It's a double bed. I can usually be found on the same side, so the left half of the mattress looks a little more worn, sags a little more deeply than the right. Symmetry is an impossibility, even here.

It's the only bedroom in the apartment—also the only room besides the bathroom to have a door. The rest of the place is a continuity: a single space that crams in a small kitchen, a living room, and a table with two chairs.

I rarely venture beyond the bedroom, unless it's to use the bathroom, warm up food in the microwave, or, in exceptional circumstances, buy something in the grocery store on the first floor of the building.

On Fridays, Josefina, a woman in her sixties, comes to give the apartment a desultory dusting and to cook a few meals: tinga de pollo, meatballs in chipotle, arroz a la mexicana, rajas con crema. Most of these dishes give me indigestion, but I look upon the discomfort as a well-deserved punishment: I've never complained to her.

Josefina in fact works for my sister, but Mariana got it into her head that I wasn't eating properly and so decided to finance these weekly visits. At first I resisted, but finally gave way.

I bought this apartment with the money that came to me two years ago from the sale of the house in Educación. Mariana used her share to make a down payment on a much more spacious apartment near her office, but I decided that I lacked the patience and perseverance needed to repay a mortgage, so bought the first place I could afford, without giving much thought to the condition of the building—in urgent need of renovation—or the neighborhood—frankly dangerous.

Had he still been alive, my father would have disapproved of the purchase of this apartment. He'd have spent hours telling me about the property bubble, the benefits of having a credit history, the practicality of buying a place where I could raise the children I don't have, when the time came. If he were still alive now, my father would disapprove of everything I do. Since he died, I'm constantly making those sorts of assumptions, as if I've taken on the office he handed down to me at his death in a dingy hospital room and now have to disapprove of myself in his name.

Something similar had happened after Teresa's death, which I first heard about on September 23, 1994, the last day of summer. It's commonly said that denial is the first phase of mourning, but for me, at the age of ten, it wasn't just the first but, for a long time, the only phase. Through a process of highly complex mental gymnastics, I managed to convince myself that not only was Teresa still alive, but that she was more attentive to what was happening in my life than she'd ever been in the past. During the first two or three years, I used to imagine her reaction to anything I did. I could almost hear her robotic voice explaining why I didn't need a certain toy, why memorizing dates was not the best way to study for my history class, why my sister's life would be more difficult than mine because she was a woman.

Those years of secretly evoking Teresa were followed by overt imitation. Between 1998 and 2001—in the full fury of adolescence—I got into the slightly forced habit of talking like her, in that neutral tone with only minimal variations that was so characteristic of her speech. At the age of fifteen or sixteen I let my hair grow and began to wear it the way she used to. But I never managed to look like Teresa: however reluctantly, I was developing my father's features, his voice, his brusque, uncouth manner.

After that imitative phase, my life continued along relatively conventional, uninteresting paths. I went to college and got a job. I had very short-lived relationships and harbored lasting grudges. I made superficial acquaintances and formed one or two friendships that were much closer but then later faded. I lived in either shared apartments or in others—as small as this one—where I was on my own. I adopted a dog that ran away one day, never to be seen again. I developed curable illnesses and chronic addictions.

Throughout all those years, I continued to see my father from time to time, and less frequently, my sister. And although I still thought about Teresa, eventually days and even weeks would pass when I managed to forget her completely, when I didn't hear her voice or imagine the way she used to smoke, leaning against the wall of the house in Educación. Days and weeks when I didn't, even once, think about Friday, September 23, 1994.

After that summer, Rat continued to be seen on the streets of Educación for some time, but following the night in the Taxqueña terminal, we never exchanged a word. Mariana forgot him almost immediately—programmatically—and began dating other boys and, later, women. Rat's reputation gradually faded after the summer of '94, which was apparently the modest peak of his popularity. His escapades were mentioned less frequently, he appeared in the Rec less often, and even his retinue of gorillas dwindled as they found new leaders. Whenever we happened to cross paths in the arcade or Los Orgullosos, I'd try to catch his eye, seeking a trace of complicity, or at least recognition that the night in Taxqueña had existed, that he'd accompanied me from my living room to the bus terminal, had helped me to cross a busy street in my local neighborhood—in my known world. But Rat either avoided me or pretended not to know who I was. He'd look at me without seeing, as if I were transparent or he had the power to see through human bodies.

For a long time I thought that maybe Rat had forgotten what happened. That, in the end, it had been less important for him than for me. He'd given me the nudge that led to one of the most formative adventures of my childhood, during the summer vacation that shaped my personality, but for Rat it had probably been one night among the many others of his teenage years, its memory blurred by an alcoholic haze. Walking with some local kid to the bus terminal and giving him a little money couldn't have had any great significance for someone generally thought to be associated with much bolder activities.

Rat disappeared from the neighborhood a few years afterward, when I was in high school. His mother spread the word that he'd gone to study abroad (the secret desire of every mother in that middle-class district during those aspirational years), but it very soon became known that he'd gotten one of his girlfriends pregnant and was selling clothes—some said marijuana too—in various street markets in the south of the city. Rat's function in Educación was speedily taken over by shadier characters who didn't brag about using temporary tattoos or drinking beer, but about smoking crack and holding up drugstores.

I next saw Rat around the middle of 2015, not long after my father was diagnosed with the advanced cancer that carried him to the grave— before my life became confined to this stained, unmade bed, to these notebooks in which I attempt to give some shape to the unspeakable, as if making origami figures with shadows. At that time, Mariana and I were alternating overnight stays in the hospital; they were exhausting shifts, as my father made use of his last weeks to reproach us incessantly for our life choices (the setbacks in my love life, my sister's lack of affection). None of us so much as mentioned Teresa's name, neither during those days of waiting nor later, at my father's funeral, or when we met the lawyer who was the executor of his will and would organize the sale of the house in Educación.

Although the insatiable tumor continued to devour his organs, there were evenings when my father's condition would seem miraculously improved, and he'd look more like the fifty-nine-year-old man he really was. He'd ask for the TV to be switched on and express unshakable opinions about anything and everything. Age had accentuated his tendency to authoritarianism: he ranted about the obstinacy of the teacher's union in relation to proposed changes to the education system, demanded that a firm hand be taken with the demonstrators in the Paseo de la Reforma, and complained about the decline of the Mexican soccer team, all in the same furious tone, in the same jaded voice. The less he knew about a topic, the more he felt justified in airing his views. Naturally, both my sister and I were incapable of remaining confined with him in that small hospital room for any length of time. If I was on duty during one of those outbursts, I'd go out for a walk through the neighboring streets and return twenty minutes later, my patience partially restored.

It was during one of those strolls that I came across Rat. In my mind, I imagined that my father's illness and the consequent revision of the past that it entailed had in some way called up or attracted Rat. Such occurrences are not unusual: we don't see a person for many years, and then one day we think about them and then run into them a few hours later in some improbable place. My life, at least, has been full of coincidences of that nature. Even so, Rat was the last person I expected to see that evening.

I didn't recognize him straight off. A long time had passed since his disappearance from the neighborhood, and he obviously wasn't the same little bastard who had dated my sister in the days immediately after Teresa's departure; he was, by then, just another overweight adult. I remember that he had a bald patch on the crown of his head that he attempted to disguise by tying his long hair back in a ponytail. My first thought was that he was someone who looked very much like a degenerate version of Rat. I guess he must have had much the same idea about me—my unshaven chin, tired eyes, and prematurely graying hair made any other assessment unlikely. He was arguing about something with a teenage girl who resembled him enough to be his daughter. I know he recognized me because, just after our eyes had met, he interrupted the angry monologue he was directing at the girl as if he were embarrassed that I might overhear him. Neither of us said anything, but we looked directly at each other for a prolonged moment, and I'm certain that we both remembered that silent parting in the bus terminal, when he left me, bewildered and tearful, with the crumpled bills in my outstretched hand, and walked hurriedly back to his house in Educación to follow his mother's orders and diligently shower before heading out again to patrol the Rec.

I've often tried to understand why Rat urged me to take any available bus. To understand why he lacked the maturity to take me home, where we'd probably have found a sober but hungover Mariana repenting her outburst, sitting in front of the TV and wondering, with increasing concern, where the hell I'd gotten to.

THE WHITE LIGHTS ILLUMINATING THE AISLE were switched off as soon as the bus departed the Taxqueña terminal to the sounds of hooting horns and the cries of street vendors. Almost at the same moment, it began to rain. I leaned against the cold window, watching the bustle of the city. The first raindrops fractured the nightscape as they trickled down the glass in unpredictable paths. What was it that determined whether a drop of water ran vertically to the bottom of the pane or zigzagged and merged with other larger droplets? Who dictated the direction those drops took during their rapid descent, guiding them toward the rivers forming in the street? I tried to follow one of them with my finger but very soon lost track of it. My breath misted the glass, contributing to the blur of everything outside the bus. The reds and greens of traffic signals, distorted by the effect of the water on the glass, were dazzling. Had Teresa boarded a bus like that one to travel to Chiapas?

A man in the uniform of another bus company, with water streaming from his hair, appeared beside the driver, and in a hoarse voice recited a speech he knew by heart after thousands of repetitions: "Good evening, ladies and gentlemen. Excuse me for bothering you during your journey. I represent the workers of the Grupo de Autotransportes Tres Estrellas union and am here to ask for your invaluable assistance. We have been on strike for three months, demanding better working conditions for our comrades. So now we're selling a variety of products, including crackers and potato chips, to raise funds for the strikers . . ." The woman sitting beside me smiled and asked if I'd like some potato chips for the journey. I was surprised; I hadn't expected any form of interaction, much less that offer. I shook my head and turned to stare again through the misted glass.

The man selling snacks walked up and down the aisle, repeating his list of products every so often, and then got off the bus with a friendly wave to the driver. The sound of the pneumatic doors of the bus closing startled me out of my reverie. The woman traveling beside me took advantage of that distraction to speak again: "Are your mommy and daddy coming to meet you in Villahermosa?" I looked at her without replying. It was impossible to calculate her age. Her smile seemed a little overdone, almost false, and she had pronounced crow's-feet around her eyes. No one was coming to meet me in Villahermosa. I'd bought the ticket at the last moment for fear that Rat would return, repenting his generosity and asking for his money back. The young man at the counter had explained that from Villahermosa it would be easy to find a bus going to San Cristóbal de las Casas or any other city in Chiapas. There was no other bus leaving from Taxqueña for Villahermosa, he said. According to him, it was my only chance of starting out for Chiapas at that time of night, unless I crossed the city to the Estación de Autobuses del Oriente.

My neighbor repeated her question, this time in an extremely famil-iar tone: "Are your mommy and daddy going to be there to meet you in Villahermosa, sweetie?" Her voice ascended toward the end of the sen-tence to an almost operatic pitch. Again, I made no reply. I was think-ing that it might be a trap. The kindness of strangers had always seemed to me suspicious. Teresa had often warned about the risks of talking to people I didn't know. To ensure that the message got through, my mother had even enlisted the figure of the Bogeyman, one of whose techniques was precisely that: talking in a kindly way to children until he hypno-tized them and put them in his bottomless sack. And if that didn't do the trick, there was also a TV campaign about such dangers that regu-larly bombarded our impressionable minds, interrupting the cartoons. Mariana would sometimes tease me by imitating the menacing ges-tures of the mustachioed man who, in those public service broadcasts, grabbed a child's shoulders with evil intentions. On such occasions, I'd remove her hand, give her a look of pure hatred, go to my bedroom, and close the door. Could the Bogeyman be a woman of uncertain age travel-ing after dark to Villahermosa, Tabasco State?

The woman was staring at me, a little surprised or annoyed that I hadn't answered her questions. "Cat got your tongue, sweetie?" she asked, trying to get a reaction. That term of affection sounded like an insult, and I decided to break my silence. "My mom will be waiting for me in Chiapas," I proudly declared. "Oh, so your journey's longer than mine. Poor little mite. You should have accepted those potato chips. It's about twelve hours just to Villahermosa." I attempted to disguise my disappointment on hearing that. Hoping to soften the blow, the woman added, "But not to worry, the bus makes two stops so we can buy food and use the restroom." I felt the urge to ask her if Villahermosa was farther away than Acapulco, my only point of reference in relation to long road trips, but then thought it would be wiser to make out I was no greenhorn and told her I was used to traveling by bus and never got hungry.

Ignoring my hostility, after a few minutes' pause, the woman started to tell me the story of her life. I tried showing my lack of interest by staring straight ahead, but that didn't seem to bother her. She'd been born in Villahermosa and had two sons living in Mexico City, whom she visited frequently. She always brought them plastic tubs of home-cooked food. Her oldest son had studied engineering and was now selling automobile parts, while the younger one was still at college, doing something related to design. They were sharing an apartment in Colonia Obrera, but the oldest was thinking of getting married and moving with his wife to a small house out in Atizapán.

As if lulled by the place names and the woman's voice—high-pitched without being irksome—I was gradually falling asleep. I made an effort to keep my eyes open but at some point that became impossible, and my head kept nodding until it finally came to rest on my neighbor's arm. She folded her sweater to make a pillow for me. I struggled against this new expression of unjustified tenderness, but sleep got the better of me and I stopped resisting, even when I felt the back of the woman's hand stroking my hair.

3

NOWADAYS, I RARELY REMEMBER MY DREAMS. Although I spend many hours in bed, my waking and sleeping lives have turned their backs on one another. Nothing of what happens while I sleep filters into my waking existence, except for a sense of angst that seems to issue from that dark place to which I escape every so often on an unfixed schedule. Maybe that's because my sleep, generally induced by narcotics, is a blind sleep. But even before I was in this condition—lying in my bed, sunk in a somnolence without boundaries or defined shape—I rarely remembered my dreams. So I'm surprised that I can recall, with such a wealth of detail, many of the important dreams I had during my childhood, particularly during that summer of 1994. It's almost as if I used up all my symbolic resources at the age of ten, and since then have had to make do with the crude literalness of the world.

That night, on the bus heading for Villahermosa, my head resting on the arm of a stranger who was stroking my hair, I dreamed that I was swimming toward an island. A few months before, I'd watched an animated version of *Robinson Crusoe*—one of those Polish or Czech cartoons Teresa permitted and that no one else at school had ever heard of—that undoubtedly influenced my dream and determined its point of departure. But my shipwreck wasn't like Crusoe's.

The dream island was surrounded by a wall, its upper part encrusted with fragments of broken bottles. It was a pretty common architectural feature in Educación at that time, and I guess it still is: people add a glass crown to their garden walls to deter possible burglars. In my dream, that glass was of the widest range of colors imaginable, like shards of the stained glass windows of ruined churches rather than broken bottles. I was swimming around the whole island—it was very large—and couldn't find a single spot to access dry land: the wall formed an impassable barrier between myself and that promised paradise. What I remember most clearly is that, in the dream, I was able to see the island from two different perspectives: on the one hand, I viewed it from my situation as a shipwrecked person hoping to come ashore; on the other, I was simultaneously able to take a bird's-eye view of it from a point fifteen feet above where I was swimming. That periscopic view displayed the walled island in all its splendor: there were trees with red fruit and a pool of thermal waters.

The dream of the walled island passed without any perceptible ending or transition into a different one. The second was also a highly visual dream. I've reconstructed and told it innumerable times since that day—possibly unconsciously adding details and interpretations, as often occurs in such cases.

My father is eating something at the dining room table of the house in Educación. I'm standing behind him, so can't see what he's eating, although from his movements I can tell that he's using his hands rather than cutlery. The dining room light flickers two or three times, as happens with all the lights in the house when there's a storm, just before they cut out completely. I slowly approach my father, hoping not to be discovered. When I'm a couple of feet from him, he turns around abruptly, and I see that he's eating a pigeon. It might be the plump pigeon in the square that I kicked when I was little, I think, but in fact it could be any pigeon or even any hen: in the dream there's insufficient detail to clarify that point. What's important is that the pigeon still has feathers: he's eating it alive or, at very least, raw and newly sacrificed. Despite the implicit horror, the scene is relatively clinical: there's no blood, and my father's expression is completely normal, as if eating a raw pigeon were the most natural thing in the world.

I woke with the sensation that we were stopping, the same sound of the pneumatic system as the doors opened, the cold night air entering the bus. With a mix of embarrassment and surprise, I lifted my head from my neighbor's lap and moved as far away from her as I could, pressing my face to the cold window.

I had a strange feeling in my guts, a sort of wooziness that I've experienced several times since then, but which, that night, on that bus, I was unable to identify. The woman traveling in the seat next to mine had also fallen asleep. I gazed in horror at the parted lips with a glint of saliva in the corners, the eyes closed in what seemed a grimace of pain. When the lights came on in the aisle, the woman slowly opened her eyes, like someone emerging from a deep trance. She looked at me, uncertain of where she was, and in her pupils I could see the passage from sleep to consciousness—as if consciousness were also a light, a light that could be switched on.

In addition to the generalized discomfort in my stomach, I noted a metallic reflux in my mouth, something like the taste of one of those old thousand-peso coins with the face of Sor Juana Inés de la Cruz. I considered asking the woman beside me for a sip of water, as she seemed to have made preparations for every eventuality, but I felt uneasy about having fallen asleep against her, about having become a vulnerable being—an injured pigeon, a failed origami figure—lying in her lap, so I said nothing and silently hoped that we were making a scheduled stop to buy food (I still had a little of the money Rat had given me).

I looked out the window, expecting to see a gas station, maybe even a bus terminal. I thought that perhaps we were in Villahermosa, that we'd reached our destination hours before we were due, very late at night, and that I'd now have to wait until dawn to board another bus that would take me to Chiapas, where I'd find Mariana and Teresa as soon as I left the terminal. Perhaps my sister and mother were aware that I was on my way and were waiting for me, holding an enormous cake with my name in sugar frosting, eager to see me, glad that the three of us had escaped the tedium of Educación. Glad, most of all, to have escaped from my father: we'd celebrate finally being free of his monstrous ordinariness, his slipper-shod evil intentions.

But outside the window, all I could see was a dusty landscape. Nopals, stones, and spindly bushes suddenly lit—as if discovered in flagrante to be bushes—by passing headlights.

The driver got out of the bus and, through the window, I watched him arguing with three men in military uniforms holding flashlights and opening the luggage compartment. I was relieved to think that I hadn't brought any bags, as I'd have been worrying about the soldiers stealing them.

From an early age, Teresa had alerted me to the inherent iniquity of anyone in uniform. On one occasion we were stopped by a patrol when she was driving Mariana and me to school. A police officer walked up to our car and, putting his head through the open window, said, "What lovely children you have, señora. You should drive more carefully. You wouldn't want anything to happen to them." She looked him straight in the face, refusing to give in to his attempt to intimidate her, and replied unsmilingly, "I haven't committed any traffic violation, but if you insist that I did, write me out a damn ticket and let me take my children to school, because I've got no intention of giving you a single peso." The officer was so surprised that he let us continue on our way without even imposing a fine, and Teresa explained that the sole aim of the local police, the judicials, and soldiers was to humiliate people and take their money, a bit like those school bullies who terrorize younger kids.

That early lesson on the role of the forces of law and order in public life was later reinforced by numerous comments and arguments about the behavior of the military in Chiapas when the uprising broke out at the beginning of '94. Teresa's "simplistic views" exasperated my father, and she used to complain that he "played down things as obvious as State repression." While those quarrels were incomprehensible to me and, it must be said, boring, belonging to a world whose codes I didn't know, the message that the military were all sons of bitches had been branded on my subconscious in the same way the primeval fear of the Bogeyman and temporary tattoos had been instilled in me as a defense mechanism by the myths circulating among children in the schoolyard.

So, as I watched the soldiers searching the luggage in the middle of the dark highway, I was certain that something bad was going to happen and turned my head to my neighbor as if seeking confirmation of this ill omen in her adult concern. I guess she realized that I was worried and tried to hide, as far as was possible, her own fears. She asked me my name (I muttered a reply) and told me that hers was María Concepción, but that everyone called her Mariconchi. That must have brought an involuntary smile to my face, because Mariconchi then asked me what was so funny. She said this in a jokey tone, as if she herself knew that her nickname was a bit ridiculous.

This exchange lightened our moods. The fact of being stopped halfway to our destination couldn't, after all, be too serious. It was probably something that happened all the time and that I wasn't aware of. Just when I was consoling myself with those thoughts, Mariconchi grabbed my hand, put her face close to mine, and whispered, "If they ask you anything, sweetie, say I'm your auntie and that your mommy and daddy have asked me to take you to Villahermosa. Got it?"

Far from calming me, this plan of action rekindled my forebodings. Who was going to ask me if I was traveling alone, if Mariconchi was my aunt, if my "mommy and daddy" were waiting for me in Villahermosa? Would the soldiers interrogate me? The possibility sent a shiver down my spine. Somehow, they must have found out about me. Was it illegal for a child to travel unaccompanied? Maybe Mariana had called the police or the army to tell them that I'd run away from home and they had mobilized their forces on land and sea until they found me in that ordinary bus, traveling through the night from dusk to dawn.

One of the soldiers boarded the bus. The aisle lights were still on and were bright enough to give a clear view of the passengers. Yet despite this, the soldier shone his flashlight on the sleepy face in the front seat. He inspected the face carefully and then moved his flashlight to the one beside it. The soldier continued along the aisle, illuminating the bleary-eyed visage of each passenger. At the third row, he lingered to order the man in a baseball cap off the bus. The man in the cap attempted to protest or ask for an explanation, but the soldier looked at him derisively and repeated his command: "Get off and wait for me outside." Another four passengers suffered the same fate before he reached us.

When he finally arrived at the row in which Mariconchi and I were sitting, I couldn't help but press myself against her. The soldier moved the beam of his flashlight from my face to hers as if comparing our features. "Is she your mom?" he asked, scrutinizing me. I tried to make my voice sound as solemn as possible before replying, "My aunt," but my mouth was dry and what came out of it was more like a hiccup or a grunt. "Both of you, outside for a check, please," said the soldier, and for a moment I thought that it was my fault, that if I'd been capable of speaking clearly, of articulating my reply with adult assurance, he wouldn't have asked us to do that.

4

THE COLD WIND ON THE HIGHWAY enveloped me as soon as I stepped onto the gravel. The bus had pulled into a rest stop, next to a shack with a sign indicating that it was a restaurant; by the look of the place, it was either closed or, more likely, abandoned. A few yards away, the headlights of an official-looking pickup were shining through the darkness. A number of passengers were already waiting, lined up on one side of the bus. They all seemed calm, joking and taking advantage of the break to stretch their legs and make small talk. That relaxed atmosphere didn't make me feel any easier; what I felt was more like pity: those poor people didn't know what they had coming, I thought. They were like cattle walking to the slaughterhouse.

I imagined the punishment that would be meted out to Mariconchi if it was discovered that we'd lied to the soldiers, if they found out that she wasn't my aunt, my mother, or any other relative. She'd surely be locked up in a dungeon like the one described in the Choose Your Own Adventure novel that I had left half-read in my bedroom. I imagined Mariconchi imprisoned in a remote tower where no one could hear her shrill cries for help. I saw myself in a jail with cold stone walls, serving a life sentence for running away from home, missing my sister, Teresa, my school friends, and Hawaiian pizza until the end of time. In my half-baked fantasy, I consoled myself by thinking that, there in the jail, I might be allowed my multicolored squares of paper to practice making the origami cranes and pagodas that had so far only ended in failure. It occurred to me that origami had been invented that way: a Japanese monk, incarcerated in some pagoda with bars on the windows, alone in his stinking cell with only a sheet of paper, which he had to fold and unfold with infinite care, aware that if he tore it, his own sanity would be rent in two.

Three more passengers carrying backpacks descended from the bus and lined up next to us. Mariconchi realized that I was shivering, so she took off her shawl and wrapped it around my chest and arms. I was no longer suspicious of her kindness. She wasn't a stranger by then; I'd known her for a few hours, which, in the context of my adventure, suddenly seemed forever.

One of the soldiers started to explain that it was a routine check, that we would be asked for our IDs and our final destinations, and that our belongings would be searched. Each of us should take our things from the baggage compartment and briefly show the contents to one of the soldiers. At the end of that explanation the officer who seemed to be in charge added, "If you aren't a guerrillero, you have nothing to worry about." Mariconchi pressed me a little closer to her thighs and leaned down to whisper in my ear in a mocking tone: "You're not a guerrillero, are you?" Those words immediately had a soothing effect. If Mariconchi was capable of cracking a joke, it was most likely that there was no danger. I wrapped the shawl a little more tightly around myself as the soldiers began to check documents and luggage.

The cold seeping through the fabric of my clothing reminded me of one Saturday, not so long before, when Teresa had decided that we should spend a few days in Lagunas de Zempoala, in Morelos State. The plan was to set off early in the morning so as to miss the worst of the traffic—the congestion used to drive my father crazy and caused arguments with Teresa that would sometimes ruin our holidays. The sensation of my father carrying me in his arms to the car woke me, but I pretended to be still asleep so I could enjoy the ever-rarer luxury of letting things happen, of being a bundle looked after by others. Forty minutes later we stopped in Huitzilac for a breakfast of quesadillas, and although—at Teresa's insistence—I'd been wrapped in a jacket, I could still feel the cold air seeping in through my pajama bottoms. My father ordered atole for us all and we sipped the thick liquid in silence. While we were eating our quesadillas, a man approached our table offering postcards of extremely poor quality, showing scenes from the Mexican Revolution, among them the famous image of Pancho Villa sitting on the presidential throne, with Emiliano Zapata beside him, after the triumphal entrance of the revolutionary troops into the capital. Teresa bought a postcard from the man, paying more than he asked (provoking a look of reproof from my father), and during the rest of the meal, she told us stories associated with that photo, describing Villa's rough-hewn character and the respect Zapata inspired in the campesinos who fought at his side.

Wrapped in Mariconchi's shawl, standing beside the bus that would take me to Villahermosa, with the beams of the soldiers' flashlights passing back and forth, I thought of that breakfast in Huitzilac, which all of a sudden seemed a blurred memory belonging to some far-distant era. In a certain sense it was a memory outside of time, as if my life were not a straight line capable of stretching back to its point of origin but something discontinuous, with ruptures that scattered the recollections across distant hills, shreds of a period that no amount of effort could faithfully reconstruct.

The beam finally rested on my face and I drew back a little, hiding in the shawl like an animal that, caught in the headlights of a car on the highway, curls up, awaiting the impact. In this case, the impact came in the form of a question, directed not at me but at Mariconchi, whose turn it was to have the flashlight shone in her face. "How old is the little girl?" The soldier in charge of the searches had a nasal twang. "Eleven," Mariconchi improvised, "and he's a boy not a girl." Beneath the shawl, I smiled, happy that she had added a year to my age and corrected the soldier in relation to my gender. But that smile quickly faded. The soldier gave a coarse, rather dissolute laugh. I'd heard a laugh like that before, but couldn't at that moment remember where. He was no more than a teenager, but his laugh was older than his years. "Wow, so he was born a fairy. Right down to the shawl!" Then he laughed again.

In the Paideia School, "fairy" was the most offensive thing one boy could call another. I'd had the bad luck of hearing it often, especially in relation to my lack of ability at sports, but I was always very careful not to react with anger: I'd force myself to ignore the insult and, at most, would smile and give my persecutors the finger, which seemed to disconcert them.

Víctor Flores, on the other hand, was an easy target. Fairy, queer, homo: there was no variant of that insult that wasn't thrown at him at least once a day. And, invariably, Víctor Flores would cry with rage, swipe his aggressor's schoolbooks to the ground, scream an interminable string of curses, and then, when it was all over, he was the one to be sent to receive his punishment from the principal—a Frenchwoman who had a perpetual smile on her face and was always dressed in red.

The image of Víctor Flores, his face smeared with snot and disfigured by rage, flitted through my mind when I heard the nasal twang of that soldier calling me a fairy. But I didn't have time to feel hurt by that insult: still riding on the crest of his inappropriate laughter, the adolescent crouched down so that his face was on a level with mine. "So, you a boy or a fairy?" His question frightened me less than the smell of his breath, something like burnt plastic or those weirdly colored liquids my father kept in the garage and every so often poured into the engine of the Tsuru. The teenage soldier looked straight at me, smiled, and I suddenly thought I remembered where I'd heard that laugh before. It was my father's laugh, the one he gave sometimes when sitting watching TV, and that I'd hear from my bedroom, from my Zero Luminosity Capsule, or while I was organizing the leaves I'd collected during the day.

Mariconchi sensed danger and tried to move me away from the soldier, hiding me behind her back. The soldier straightened up and slapped her lightly, more to sow the seeds of fear than to inflict pain. Mariconchi raised both hands to her face. One of the passengers who had already been checked attempted to intervene, but a second soldier approached with a menacing expression, raising his rifle as if he were going to hit him with it.

The adolescent soldier crouched down again in front of me, breathing his solvent smell in my face. "Let's see if you're a girl or a fairy." I was petrified, and Mariconchi, frozen with impotence, was crying silently without moving a single muscle, like those miraculous Virgins in churches.

The adolescent soldier unwound Mariconchi's shawl and proceeded to frisk me from the calves upward, as if checking for a weapon. At that moment, there wasn't a single thought in my head. For the first time, my mind was a blank, like a sheet of paper with absolutely no creases. The second soldier, who stood watching a few steps away, intervened in a tone intended to sound casual but that held a clear note of tension: "That's enough." The adolescent soldier removed his hands as if he were coming out of a trance or had been burned. He straightened up once more and advanced toward the next passenger in the line, whom he searched mechanically before asking for his ID.

I didn't hear his laugh again so was never able to confirm that it was similar to my father's, but that notion—or rather, that intuition—secreted itself in a dark corner of my being, like an animal lying in wait to pounce on its prey.

Everything suddenly seemed more silent, like an engine had been turned off somewhere. Mariconchi hugged me as tightly as she could, wrapping her shawl around me again. That hug was slightly painful. I closed my eyes and allowed her to continue, but there was a rigidity in my body that made any real embrace impossible, as if I'd been converted into a piece of splintered wood. I wanted to be inside my Zero Luminosity Capsule, or lying on my bed surrounded by failed origami cranes, with the sound of Mariana's music filtering through the wall. I wanted to be in Huitzilac, eating a breakfast of quesadillas with Teresa; listening to her monotonous voice, barely rising to enthusiasm as she spoke of the illustrious men of the past. Most of all, I wanted to be with her in Chiapas, walking through the mist along a path, guided by the man with the pipe and balaclava.

When I opened my eyes, I was sitting in my seat on the bus, next to the window. We were once again traveling at a steady speed, and it suddenly occurred to me that it had all been a nightmare. I had no clear memory of how the whole episode at the checkpoint had ended, no memory of boarding the bus with Mariconchi and falling asleep, and no idea of how much time had elapsed since then. What seemed most likely was that it had been a horrible dream, induced by sinister stories about the Bogeyman, by the Choose Your Own Adventure novels, by Teresa's disappearance, and by the grave tone in which Rat had warned me about the war in Chiapas.

I felt a coldness in my legs and thought that it was due to the air conditioning, but when I looked down I realized that my pants were wet. The odor of urine was slight but unmistakable, and even though I was ashamed of that smell, I consoled myself with the thought that it was familiar and organic, unlike the chemical smell of solvent on the adolescent soldier's breath.

At my side, Mariconchi was staring straight ahead, apparently ignoring me, as if we'd never exchanged a single word. Or rather, as if she were sleeping with her eyes open—Mariana had told me about similar cases: sleepwalkers whose unblinking eyes were always wide open.

A little later, I noticed a lightening of the horizon outside the window, and after a while the sun came up. By that time the urine on my pants had dried, although the tenuous smell persisted. The passengers were waking up as if nothing had happened, as if that nighttime halt in the middle of the highway had been, for them too, a vivid dream they would forget in the course of a few hours, as the sun warmed the world.

5

IF I HAD THE WILL TO LEAVE THIS BED, I'd like to take a taxi to the Taxqueña terminal and, once there, board the same bus bound for Villahermosa that I took twenty-three years ago. Perhaps in that way, through the ritual of repetition, the ramifications of that night—of that summer—would be obliterated. Perhaps then the dream about my father and the pigeon, the laugh of the teenage soldier, Mariconchi's absorbed expression, the somber forebodings that welled up as I watched the sun rise that morning; perhaps all that would become a closed book, water under the bridge, a past history that no longer affects me. But I know that going to Taxqueña now and taking that same bus would be no use. It wouldn't do any good. First I have to write the story through to the end, fill this spiral-bound notebook with my scribblings to the very last page, drop it by the bed, open the next notebook, and continue writing until that one, too, is full. Not because writing is an act of salvation, but because there's no other way I can tell myself the things I don't even dare think when I'm alone. Only when I've written it all down will I be able to look at myself in the mirror and not see the face of someone else, the other that stalks me from within.

Josefina—the woman who, on Mariana's instructions, cleans my apartment—turned up this morning, so I guess it must be Friday. I spoke with her for a long time, or rather, she spoke, and I listened from my bed. Her voice was drowned out from time to time by the noise of dishes being washed, but I was able to deduce from the context what I'd missed. She told me a sad, complicated story about feuds between neighbors and threats made by the local political boss.

As she was leaving, Josefina told me that I should get in touch with Señora Mariana—as she calls my sister—more often. What had she seen or heard in my sister's home to cause her to offer me that advice? Was Mariana all right? Had she broken up with her partner after four years of conjugal bliss? Was it, in fact, my life, what happens in this apartment, that led her to believe that I need to talk to someone?

Whatever the case, I decide to contact Mariana. I don't call her on the phone, that would be going too far; instead I send a message: "Remember when I kicked a pigeon in the square?" Her reply takes several hours, and arrives as night is falling: "Ha ha. You cried for three days."

Despite the apparent coolness of its content, her message calms me for a while. I like the way Mariana is never condescending toward me, even though she knows that I'm in a fragile, disturbed state of mind, even though she's aware that I seldom leave my bed. Criticizing me, laughing at my way of dramatizing events, is her way of showing affection. I've been at peace with that fact for many years.

When Mariana left home at the age of eighteen it seemed to me an unpardonable betrayal. My father took advantage of the situation to convert my sister's bedroom into a utility room, in which he stored a broken television set and an exercise bike he only ever used three times. That dusty room seemed to represent everything that separated my father from his daughter.

Without the grease of everyday life together, my relationship with Mariana also began to show signs of rust. Later, she cut herself off from my father completely for several years due to an argument, the details of which no one ever explained to me. At that time I was contending with the normal adolescent conflicts—intensified by my mania for trying to resemble my dead mother—and didn't have the maturity to restore the fraternal relations Mariana had unilaterally broken off.

Only my father's unexpected diagnosis of cancer, two years ago, brought us together again. Our first meetings, in the hospital cafeteria, were a little awkward. Initially, Mariana and I opted for a sort of unnatural formality; like former workmates, we caught up on the basics of our lives without going into details or alluding to feelings. My father's illness was, naturally, the theme we most frequently returned to. We commented on his prognosis, the treatments the doctors proposed without convincing either him or us of their efficacy, the general conditions in the hospital. Then we'd sit in uncomfortable silence, sipping stewed coffee from our polystyrene cups.

Gradually both Mariana and I relaxed, perhaps worn down by the weariness my father's cancer induced in us. A sort of mutual understanding was restored between us. She began to tease me again, like when we were kids, and on several occasions I fruitlessly attempted to get her to talk about Teresa and the summer of '94. "Forget it, little bro. That was a long time ago, none of it matters now." But however much Mariana refused to acknowledge the weight of the past in her life, it was obvious that Teresa's premature death had affected her as much as it had me, although in different—maybe even opposite—ways. What in Mariana became rage, inspiration, a motor that gave her life direction and force, had hollowed me out, like a subterranean river eroding my essentially feeble adult normality.

After leaving the house in Educación, Mariana graduated from college with top grades and started out on a successful career as a government policy consultant. I didn't tell her at that time, and still haven't—it would be a weird thing to include in a text message—but it's always been clear to me that something of Teresa's undaunted critical spirit, her way of taking things seriously, lives on in Mariana.

For my part, I find it more difficult to identify what I inherited from Teresa. Despite all my efforts to be like her, my social conscience has never developed to the level of making me feel passionate about the things that mattered deeply to her—and now matter deeply to Mariana. I even have the impression that, with time, my features have become increasingly less like my mother's. And, as I've already said, my voice has never—in its natural state—had that same neutral tone.

For a time I convinced myself that I'd inherited Teresa's analytical ability, her way of questioning and distrusting everything. I now realize that I was never sufficiently distrustful.

On the other hand, I have my father's eyebrows and chin, his explosive temper, and, it seems, a pathetic unwillingness to move from my bed, even for the end of the world.

In material terms, I inherited everything from him, including the money I used to buy this apartment and these spiral-bound notebooks in which I write. When I was emptying the house in Educación I found scarcely anything that might have belonged to Teresa beyond a few photos, some books on political theory, and two letters: the one she left on my father's night table when she went away and another, which she mailed to him from Chiapas shortly before her death.

6

THE SUN WAS WELL UP IN THE SKY when the driver made a stop and explained that we had fifteen minutes to purchase provisions and use the restrooms. The fact that we took this break made me think that it was still a long way to Villahermosa, but, guessing my concern or reading it in my face, Mariconchi assured me that we were nearly there, with at most two hours to go.

My spirits had flagged after the episode at the military checkpoint—I still wasn't completely sure it had actually happened. In the light of day, I was convinced that my journey made no sense. I'd never find Teresa. First, because I didn't know where she was; my plan to search for the man with the pipe and balaclava until I discovered her too—there, in the warzone of the Chiapas jungle—began to seem embarrassingly naive. I was hungry, I wanted to change my clothes and leave behind the smell of piss.

Mariconchi asked me if I had enough to buy something for breakfast, and I extracted from my pocket what little remained of the money Rat had given me. "You hold on to that, sweetie. This is on me. After all, we're old friends now," she said, and it gave me a tremendous sense of peace to corroborate that my perception of time was shared: we'd just passed through the longest night in history. Even the military checkpoint (the chemical smell on the soldier's breath, the echo of his laugh) felt like a distant memory, like something that had happened during the previous school year—an old story everyone already knew and no longer mentioned.

While Mariconchi was standing in line to buy food, I went to the restroom and locked myself in one of the stalls. The toilet was blocked and there was shit-stained paper on the floor. Being very careful not to touch anything, I took off my pants and then my briefs. The moment I threw the briefs into a corner of the stall, I remembered that they had a name tag: a name tag Teresa had sewn onto the inside of the waistband. I considered retrieving them, taking them with me. It would be a mistake to leave a clue to my identity in that stall. As my life appeared to have become a Choose Your Own Adventure book, it was time I started thinking like one of the heroes of those stories.

On the other hand, the briefs were revolting, and I was ashamed of them. The urine had dried, marking out strange continents on the white fabric. A compromise solution occurred to me: I picked up the briefs, pulled off the name tag, and put it in my pocket. Then I threw them back down among the filth. I left the stall and washed my hands with the satisfaction of knowing that I'd acted wisely. I'd covered my tracks. No one would be able to trace me. True, my pants were still a little stiff and smelled of dry piss, but I felt freer. I had neither briefs bearing my full name nor a definite destination. I had no home, no family, no friends. The distinction between vacations and school had lost its meaning. I could have started afresh at that point, changed my identity and persuaded Mariconchi to adopt me: her hugs were warm and she used terms of affection that would have been impossible to imagine on Teresa's lips. I could have invented a new life for myself, made to the measure of my desires and frustrations. A life in Villahermosa, Tabasco State, in the humidity and tropical sunlight.

If I'd been able to choose a name for my new self, I wouldn't have had to give it a second thought: Úlrich González. That was the name of a boy who had turned up in Paideia in the middle of the academic year only to then disappear, just as unexpectedly, two weeks later. Úlrich was pale and sickly. The rumor was that his parents traveled a lot. No one at school had managed to become either a friend or rival of Úlrich González, and everyone seemed to forget his existence the moment he stopped coming to class, but his name remained on the register for several months, and some absentminded teachers would read it out as if he were still one of us. That repetition had caused the mysterious appellation to be etched deeply in my memory, and I even sometimes repeated it to myself quietly as a sort of invocation: "Úlrich González, Úlrich González."

If I took on that new identity, if I became Úlrich González of Villahermosa, I'd do things differently. To start with, I'd try to play soccer properly, take more interest in sports, be one of the group of students everyone wanted to be friends with, the celebrities of my school. In the afternoons, I'd return home smiling and excited, bursting with stories to tell my adoptive mother, Mariconchi. Úlrich González would be the most popular boy in Villahermosa, perhaps even in the whole of Tabasco State. I'd finally have a girlfriend, and it would be to her alone, in a moment of blind passion following our first kiss, that I would reveal the truth about my past: that I wasn't Úlrich, that I'd assumed that name at the age of ten in the shit-strewn restroom of a service station, after running away from my home in Colonia Educación, Mexico City, on a secret mission to rescue my mother, who was trapped in a cruel, bloody war that she had joined from pure, unadulterated heroism. My girlfriend would gaze at me incredulously for a few seconds, but then she'd put her arms around my neck and say that she'd always known, or suspected it; said that beneath the personality of the likeable, sporty Úlrich González of Villahermosa lay a dark, indecipherable secret that had captivated her from the instant we'd met.

Mariconchi's voice broke into my daydreams: "Here you are. I don't know if you like spicy food, but I bought you a tamal with green chili sauce." I didn't in those days eat spicy food, couldn't stand it, and disliked the color green. At mealtimes, Teresa always used to say that adding sauce to food was a bad habit as it masked the taste of everything else. It was, fundamentally, another of the ways she drew a line between herself and my father, who used to smother any dish from eggs to rice in industrial quantities of habanero chili sauce. I, of course, used that disagreement to take Teresa's side, the side I always took. But maybe Úlrich González could stand or even positively liked spicy food, and that was a good moment to start to behave the way Úlrich would. "Thanks," I said, and tried to grasp Mariconchi's hand, but she drew it away as if she was beginning to weary of taking responsibility for me, or was frightened by that unexpected familiarity.

Her snub didn't really bother me. Quite the reverse: the fact that my traveling companion was displaying a degree of hostility made her much more interesting. Suddenly Mariconchi had ceased to be the soft-hearted, chatty mother who goes around calling everyone "sweetie" and had become a woman of moods and nuances, a brave woman— like my mother, like Mariana—who had challenged the irrational violence of the adolescent soldier in order to care for a strange child, some unknown Úlrich.

We boarded the bus again and took our seats. The shawl Mariconchi had lent me at the checkpoint lay screwed up in a ball on my seat, like a reminder that everything that had occurred at the checkpoint had been real, not a nightmare.

We ate our tamales in silence, picking away at them with plastic forks and scattering crumbs around us. I found it almost impossible to eat the chili. It felt as if my tongue were being scalded, but in some way that self-inflicted pain seemed purifying, redemptive, soothing. My nose was streaming and I began to hyperventilate. Mariconchi seemed to be aware of my distress but said nothing. I noticed that she was even making a conscious effort not to look at me, to stare across the aisle at the obese couple on the other side who had bought enormous quantities of snacks, cookies, and sodas.

The bus advanced more rapidly, as if the sun and the imminence of our arrival had raised its spirits. The reality of my situation began to hem me in on all sides: it wasn't now viable to change my identity: Mariconchi wouldn't accept me into her life as Úlrich González, and I would never have a good, empathetic girlfriend in Villahermosa, Tabasco State.

And I wasn't even sure if I wanted to continue my journey to Chiapas. The episode with the soldiers had changed everything. The adult world was more brutal and terrifying than I'd supposed in Taxqueña, before embarking on the most perilous adventure of my short life. If I continued to Chiapas, new checkpoints would await me, new humiliations. I was unready for any of that. Deceived by a rather portable conception of Mexican geography, I'd undertaken that journey without the necessary preparations. I hadn't even brought my backpack. I hadn't even brought my Choose Your Own Adventure book or my water bottle.

"Your mom's not going to be there to meet you in Chiapas, is she?" asked Mariconchi out of the blue when she'd finished her tamal. It was a rhetorical question: she knew I'd lied to her. Mothers know these things. I shook my head in shame. "Have you run away from home?" she asked in the same wary tone. I said I had. I tried to explain that my mom was in fact in Chiapas, but Mariconchi gestured me to be silent. She stared again at the obese couple on the other side of the aisle, weighing up her options. Finally she came to a conclusion: "When we get to

Villahermosa we're going to talk to your mommy and daddy, sweetie. Let's see if they can come to collect you."

I imagined the scolding my father would give me: he'd look grave, attempt to reason with me, speak very slowly and clearly, explain the risks I'd run in going off like that. But the longer he spoke, the more fired up he'd get; he always did. From explaining, he'd quickly progress to shouting. The patient, carefully thought-out language would warp into an explosion of uncontrolled emotion. I knew his tones of voice well, the registers of his language. They were mine too: I was also incapable of having a sensible discussion (as Teresa had been able to, as Mariana still can). I couldn't at that time—and still can't—tolerate someone thinking differently to me or doing something that annoys me. I'd get steamed up, lose my grip. So my father's shouting didn't alarm me: it was my shouting, and it was also my unstable, explosive irrationality.

If Teresa had been at home, I'd have been much more scared of the payback. She'd have taken her time, carefully chosen the words that would most profoundly shake me: "I'm disappointed in you," or "I'm very sad to see that you can't be left alone, even for a moment." Devastating words that always went straight to the mark, that would wash away my fragile construction of pretexts like a wave that reduces the most complex sandcastles to nothing. Would I ever achieve that level of precision in my own use of words, that ninja state of language Teresa used to brandish before us, her children, like a light, finely honed sword?

Maybe Teresa had in fact returned home that very night, while I was wetting my pants on the bus, I thought. Such magical coincidences were always occurring in the books I read: a child who rescues his best friend from a cave at the precise instant that the roof is about to collapse on top of him; the prince who, after years away at war, arrives at his father's deathbed at the very moment he's uttering his last words.

I allowed that fantasy free rein: if Teresa had returned, there would be no scolding or "I'm disappointed in you"—it would be a long, long hug. My mom's voice would finally sound affectionate, it would quiver with emotion, and then I'd excitedly show her the progress I'd made in the Japanese art of origami; I'd tell her about Mariconchi, and how I'd courageously protected that frightened woman from the bullying and humiliation of the soldiers on a godforsaken highway in the middle of the night. And Teresa would listen to my stories as never before: with genuine interest, with the respect of someone listening to an equal.

My father, in the meantime, would be serving us lemonade like a diligent butler; or he'd be watching TV, absorbed like the infant he really was, and I'd finally be the adult male in the household: I'd move into Teresa's bedroom despite Mariana's irate protests, despite the protests of my father and the man with the pipe and balaclava.

7

OF VILLAHERMOSA, I REMEMBER LITTLE. I'd never before experienced anything like the heat that hit me when I descended from the bus, not even in Acapulco. The change from the air conditioning of the vehicle to the dense humidity of the terminal was so extreme, it was as if we'd passed from the atmosphere of one planet to another. Even the force of gravity seemed different: it took more effort to lift your feet from the ground. For an instant I considered the possibility that Villahermosa was, in fact, another planet. A planet on which everyone said "sweetie" and "mommy and daddy" and which was considerably nearer to the sun than Colonia Educación.

When Mariconchi had extracted her shapeless, unwieldy bag from the luggage compartment, she looked at me with a touch of hostility. Perhaps she wasn't used to lying, and so she thought it had been unforgivable of me to have told her that Teresa would be coming to meet me in Chiapas, to have given her to understand that my journey had the complete approval of my parents. By contrast, in my home, lying was just something that came naturally to us. For Mariana, Teresa, and me, lies were no more important than, for instance, alliteration—and were employed with much greater frequency. This was not, however, the case with my father. It annoyed him when we told lies; whenever he discovered us being untruthful, there would be an eruption of anger that lasted several days.

Mariana's lies were, I have to admit, the best. I've always admired her ability to instantaneously come up with a really complex series, often in the form of pretexts.

On one occasion, my sister was planning to go to a party where there would be no adult supervision, organized by some students in their final year of high school. I knew about it because I used to eavesdrop on her telephone conversations, my ear pressed to the wood of her bedroom door. In order to gain permission, she told Teresa that her friend Citlali was hosting a pajama party. At nine in the evening, Teresa decided to call Citlali's house to see how everything was going, and of course my sister wasn't there, and hadn't been there at all that day. Half an hour later, Mariana herself called, and an extremely annoyed Teresa dropped one of her emotional bombshells of the "I'm disappointed in you" variety. But my sister didn't break under the pressure. She invented the tale that there was another Citlali, whom she'd never before mentioned. She was a younger, quieter girl who had had polio in her childhood and so walked with a bad limp due to a dislocated hip. As a triumphal end to the pack of lies she'd just produced, she passed the phone to a man who claimed to be the disabled Citlali's father, and told Teresa that everything was fine.

I don't know if Teresa believed that or any other of Mariana's many falsehoods, but she pretended to, and my theory is that she was training us to lie effectively: she only scolded us if the lie didn't hold water, lacked detail, or was frankly idiotic. (Mine were generally all three. When I later decided to study literature, it was with the secret desire to improve those lies, even though by then it was already too late.)

In some way, Teresa's disappearance was one more lesson in that everlasting fiction class that was her life. She'd played the role of the spouse, mother, and suburban housewife for sixteen years: a lie she'd clung to with tooth and nail, with her whole body, until she herself believed it. I don't know if it was due to the Zapatista uprising in Chiapas, the naturally downward slope her marriage was on, or—more generally—the advent of a Truth with a capital T, but during that summer of '94, Teresa's lie fell apart. Or perhaps it would be better to say that it had been silently disintegrating for many years and finally, that Tuesday at midday, came tumbling down.

From the perspective offered by the intervening two decades, I now guess that when she got off the bus, Mariconchi wasn't exactly angry with me. True, my lie had put her in an awkward position, but I imagine that to some extent she considered herself responsible for my fate. What's more, she may perhaps have felt guilty that an unnamed soldier had traumatized me for life while I was in her care, as would appear to be indicated by the fact that I'd pissed my pants at the age of ten. How was she going to explain to my father that his son was with her, five hundred miles away, on a planet nearer to the sun where the force of gravity was different?

After leaving the bus terminal, we took a cab to Mariconchi's house, and I remember being surprised that it was a normal car, with four doors, and not one of the ubiquitous Beetles with no front passenger seat that abounded in the streets of the capital.

Mariconchi's house was painted in the most surprising colors. The front door was navy blue, the living room walls were apricot, the kitchen was a pale green, and there was a small interior patio with clay-colored tiles. The large number of ornaments on every available surface made the house a kitsch baroque nightmare. On shelves, porcelain dolls stood beside small vases commemorating weddings and baptisms. It was completely unlike any other house I'd ever entered. I immediately assumed that this was the predominant style in Villahermosa.

Over and above the excessive ornamentation, there was a disturbing element in that house; it seemed to be preserved like a museum rather than being a lived-in space. I knew from her first monologue, when we were just leaving the Taxqueña terminal, that my host's sons lived in Mexico City, but I didn't remember hearing anything about a partner, and I posed my question with the innocent directness typical of those days: "Where's your husband?" Mariconchi stroked my hair before replying, and it was as if she'd called me "sweetie" for the umpteenth time, but on this occasion with a gesture rather than words. "He passed on three years ago."

I'd always envied children who felt relatively confident around adults, who spoke the full range of the polite language of social encounters and were praised by teachers and aunts for having "very good manners." Teresa had never trained us to avoid awkward questions, repeat formulaic courtesies, or utilize the blandest euphemism to suit the occasion. That is the only explanation for the fact that, despite my relatively morbid taste in reading matter (including the Choose Your Own Adventure books) and my reasonable performance in the language class, I still, at the age of ten, had no clear notion of the meaning of the verb "pass on." At home, we simply said "die": my father's father had died before I was born, and Kurt, Mariana's red-eared terrapin, had died a few months before the death of the singer it had been named after, but no one around me had ever, as far as I knew, *passed on*. From Mariconchi's tone, I could tell that passing on wasn't something good, yet by a process of association I would find impossible to reconstruct today, it seemed to me that her husband must be some form of vegetable in a wheelchair whom she visited from time to time in a hospital.

While I was lost in those linguistic conundrums (omitting to express any form of condolence or regret), Mariconchi produced a pen and paper from a drawer and asked me to note down my home phone number, which I did without hesitation, since I had an inkling that her generosity and patience were reaching their limits. She then disappeared for a moment and returned with a towel, a T-shirt, and a pair of shorts that looked six or seven sizes too large for me. "Give me your clothes and go take a shower. I'll talk to your daddy and then wash your things so you're clean as a new pin when he comes to get you." I immediately realized that carrying out her request would imply standing naked in front of her, and I felt myself blush. Mariconchi must have spotted that blush because she laughed. It made me a little less nervous to see the worried expression she'd worn since early that morning fleetingly disappear.

I took off my clothes in the bathroom and, after wrapping myself in the towel she'd given me, handed my pants and T-shirt to Mariconchi. I was worried that she might ask about my briefs—discarded among the filthy litter of the service station restroom—but either she didn't notice their absence or guessed it was a sensitive topic and said nothing.

Back in the bathroom, I imagined the telephone call that was about to be made. My father would be desperately searching for me. He'd surely have brought in the police or would be in jail for accidentally killing Rat while torturing him for information about my whereabouts. Mariana would be feeling guilty, like the time when she tied me to the gate with a bicycle lock and then lost the key. The house in Educación would be filled with reporters, and my smiling face would appear that day, along with those of other missing children, on the public-service break-bumpers on Channel 5.

Whatever the case, the phone would scarcely have time to ring in the tense silence of the living room before my father leaped to answer it. I imagined his surprise on hearing Mariconchi's kindly voice, her speech peppered with diminutives, the tale of our bus journey, the revelation that I was safe in her house, taking a shower, and, perhaps, the treacherous accusation that I'd wet my pants. I imagined the haste with which my sister would try to grab the handset from him, the police officer advising caution as his team traced the call. But what I couldn't imagine was any possible ending to that conversation. What plan would be agreed on? Would my father take a plane to Villahermosa, Tabasco State, before noon to personally drag me back home? Would they arrange for Mariconchi herself to put me on a bus back to the capital, thus exposing me to the risk of the adolescent soldier with chemical breath humiliating me again that night? Would Mariana attempt to assuage her guilt by offering to come to Villahermosa to fetch me? After all, she'd supposedly been looking after me when I disappeared. And the most important question of all: Would they ask Mariconchi to tell me that Teresa had come home?

I stood for quite a while under the tepid stream, stronger than in Educación, without soaping myself down, feeling the water massage my back.

I recalled an occasion when I'd woken up feeling ill, with a cough, difficulty breathing, and an indefinite pain in my chest. The pediatrician I usually saw was on vacation, so Teresa took me to another, recommended by someone who worked with my father at the bank.

The doctor was an elderly man with a military bearing and brusque manner. After examining me and scrawling a prescription for cough syrup, he turned to Teresa and, in a grave tone, said: "What this child needs is for his father to wake him up at six in the morning and put him under a cold shower. If he gets into that habit early in life, he'll never fall ill and will be a stronger, more hard-working boy." Teresa smiled, thanked the doctor for his advice, and left his office. I was pretty surprised by the proposed regimen, which had very little resemblance to the remedies prescribed by my usual pediatrician.

Once we were in the car, Teresa looked solemnly into my eyes and, imitating the doctor's voice, said, "What this child needs is to shower in ice-cold water." Then she let loose a laugh that she appeared to have been holding back for some time. I'd never before seen her do anything like that; imitating someone and then laughing, I mean. It was in complete contrast to the absolute seriousness she normally projected. I laughed too; nervous rather than genuinely amused.

When Teresa had pulled into traffic, changing the mood, I asked why the doctor had said that I ought to shower in cold water, and Teresa's answer only served to further disconcert me: "Because he believes that if we get you out of bed early and put you under a cold shower, you won't deplete your energy levels masturbating. He must be a religious fanatic." I made no reply. What could I have said? I was ashamed by the doctor's insinuation and annoyed with my mother for having explicitly voiced it.

8

A PART OF ME KNOWS that my situation is unsustainable. After two years of living on the inheritance I received after my father's death (or at least what was left of it when I bought the place where I now live), it's beginning to be clear that I'll have to look for a job, go out into the world, and take up my life where I left off when, in the uninhabited house in Educación, surrounded by cardboard boxes, I searched through my father's papers and read Teresa's two letters. But for the moment there's no way I can even think of facing up to the frenzied activity of the city's streets. The very idea makes me feel more ungrounded than usual.

My father's phone call, two and a half years ago, had taken me by surprise. We'd gotten into the habit of exchanging text messages approximately one Sunday a month, using only the innocuous formulas that rule fleshless father-son relationships: "How are things?" "Just chilling out over here." "Are you going to watch the game?" "No, I don't even know who's playing," and so on.

A call from him, at ten in the evening, and to top it all on a Thursday, was an anomaly that presaged problems.

After a little beating about the bush, he told me that for months he'd been feeling unwell, constantly tired. His condition had gotten much worse in recent weeks: he no longer had the energy to go for a morning run before his eight-hour shift at the office. I made no response, sensing that his news hadn't finished there: my proud father wouldn't have called to tell me that he was getting old, weak, and sickly.

There followed further digressions—the farce that was left-wing politics in Mexico City and the price of gas—until he worked himself up to continuing his confession. A few weeks before, he'd visited the doctor and had been sent to have several tests done. That very morning he'd gone back with the results and had been told that he had cancer.

He didn't say "a tumor," he said "cancer." His tone in pronouncing that word sounded deeply strange, as if he'd been repeating it aloud for hours, until he'd emptied it of all meaning.

I was standing in the kitchen of the rented apartment where I lived at that time, when I still had a job, personal projects, and ambitions. I asked my father to give me a moment and went to my bedroom. My roommate wasn't home; in fact there was no one else in the whole house, but I felt the need for greater privacy, so I closed the door behind me and sat on the bed.

I asked my father if they were going to operate, or start with chemotherapy. He sighed and said, "There's no point." I had the feeling that he was going to add something further and waited, but he'd already said everything he had to say. He'd never been much of a conversationalist.

"Have you spoken to Mariana?" I managed to ask before he hung up. "What for? She's not interested. She's fine as she is, with her girlfriend, her job, and her stuff." The anger in his voice covered a cry for help: he was asking me to act as an intermediary, to give the news to my sister.

Naturally, that wasn't a phone call I had any desire to make. Mariana and I weren't very close at that time. But whereas my father hadn't been invited to her wedding the year before, I had. And Katia, her wife, had treated me with warm familiarity, constantly demonstrating that Mariana had told her a lot about our childhood, about how important we were to each other after Teresa's death.

And my father was, and had always been, a troglodyte. I'd become inured to his lack of tact, his rather brusque way of saying just what was on his mind, but Mariana found it almost impossible to grin and bear it. My father's manner drove her crazy, gave rise to a form of rage bordering on disgust. Any conversation between them about the cancer might go horribly wrong if I didn't intervene. My father was capable of using the call to complain about her coldness, about not being invited to her wedding, being refused the recognition he deserved for having single-handedly put his two children through college (public and free, but he wouldn't mention that). And Mariana was capable of lashing out and saying that she hadn't invited him because she didn't want to feel ashamed of him in front of her friends; in the heat of the argument, my sister might even have been capable—and not for the first time—of insinuating that my father was alone because neither Teresa nor anyone else could stand him, which was, when you came down to it, true.

When I rang, Mariana was more upbeat than usual. She spent several minutes telling me about the vacation she and Katia were planning to the nature reserve on Isla Holbox. I asked if they had already made a hotel reservation, anticipating the disappointment of having to cancel the trip if my father were to die just before they left. The reservations had been made.

Plucking up my courage, I finally broached the subject. "I spoke to my father just now." "So what did the fascist pig have to say for himself?" However harsh it might sound, "fascist pig" was the almost affectionate term we used between ourselves to refer to him. "He's dying. He's riddled with cancer." After a few moments' silence, Mariana replied in a flat voice, similar to Teresa's monotone: "I'll have to cancel the trip." I guess she was hoping that I'd contradict her, say, "Don't worry. You go ahead, I'll sort everything out and take you to the cemetery when you get back so you know the location of the grave you'll never visit." But I said nothing, and Mariana and Katia canceled their vacation.

Eight days later, my father had been admitted to the hospital and was connected to a morphine drip. Although he'd always said he wanted to "die peacefully at home," as soon as he found out about the cancer, the pain kicked in, as if the illness had been waiting to be given a name to proliferate and demonstrate its brutality. It was immediately apparent that he'd spend the rest of his days—which would surely be few—in that bed in a hospital in Colonia Roma. And no one wants their father to die alone, when the nursing staff are changing shifts, with Jell-O stains on his clothes, and a game show on the TV in his room, so I began to spend my days with him at the hospital, making occasional trips to the house in Educación to bring him fresh clothes, magazines, and his address book.

To be honest, I wasn't expecting to share the burden with Mariana. I thought she'd turn up at normal visiting hours, sometimes alone, sometimes with Katia, and would promise to keep an eye on text messages so she could help me with the funeral arrangements when the time came.

But on the first night, she appeared carrying a gym bag containing a toothbrush and a change of clothing, and told me we could do shifts—she'd warned them at work that she wasn't going to be around the whole day—and I could go home. I didn't go. That evening, we stayed together in the hospital, and during the night went down to the cafeteria a few times, where the flame of our relationship was rekindled. We spoke of everything except Teresa. Unlike me, Mariana preferred not to touch on delicate subjects.

During the following three months, that hospital became the living room of my house, and the cafeteria, my office. My father's insurance policy covered the expenses of a private room, and no one was hurrying him to vacate his bed (to go home when he was a little better, or to the grave when he could no longer bear the pain). In that bed, my father was slowly consumed by the cancer, while Mariana and I aged, either in the chair at his side or walking the corridors of the hospital when insomnia sank its teeth into our backs.

My father got hooked on the morphine in a matter of hours. He passed so quickly into an idyllic state that I was surprised he hadn't already developed some other addiction—apart, that is, from his obligatory tequila before dinner and, in recent years, his nighttime Valium. The doctors did their best to keep the dosage low, first arguing that he might accidentally take too much and then, when they realized the weakness of that argument in such circumstances, that my father's insurers would be unwilling to pay for such large quantities of opiates.

As had always happened when life attempted to prohibit him something, my father's solution was high-handedness: he sent me off to collect a wad of bills he'd stashed in the house and ordered me to use the money to bribe "the damned head nurse" or go to a drugstore and buy the stuff. I explained that we'd need a prescription, and he spent the following days insisting to the downy-cheeked physician that he had to have that document because the hospital morphine cost an arm and a leg. The doctor finally gave way and I was able to buy two types of morphine: injectable and in pill form (to cover all eventualities), so that my father could enjoy that last pleasure life had conceded him as he himself saw fit.

I sometimes think that if it hadn't been for the morphine, my father would have died in a matter of weeks. Instead, he survived for almost three months, floating on an ever higher and denser cloud of opiates until any distinction between sleep and death was hairsplitting. Only then did he have the courage to finally die.

Two and a half years on, my existence is, like his during those months, restricted to the width of a bed. From here, in the tangle of my sweat-stained sheets, accompanied only by these notes—by these notebooks in which I scribble as a form of salvation, and these words I weave together in search of meaning—I'm able to understand the infinite pleasure my father must have experienced on discovering, after a whole life of work, the sweet honey of immobility.

One evening at the hospital, while waiting for the arrival of the doctor to carry out his daily examination, I asked my dad why he'd continued going to the office during those months, when he was already feeling tired and ill, had found blood in his stools, and had to take cabs everywhere because he got dizzy when he drove himself; why he hadn't visited the doctor earlier or called me to say that he wasn't well, that he had symptoms; why he hadn't asked me to go with him to the hospital. "I don't know," he responded grouchily. "I had a lot of outstanding business." I imagine that when he did finally consult the doctor, someone else immediately replaced him at the bank and took over the outstanding business that couldn't be put off and weighed so heavily on his mind. He was a wholly dispensable employee. Perhaps the only way my father had of feeling important was to behave as if he actually were.

A number of his colleagues came to see him in the hospital while we were waiting for him to get around to dying, but none of them seemed particularly close to him. They used to tell him dull stories, pretending they were funny, pass on best wishes from the secretaries, bring flowers that would probably remain fresh longer than his body, and then depart, leaving behind the smells of aftershave, tequila, and dry-cleaned shirts.

Apparently, during his fifty-nine years of life, my father had never formed any close relationships or had intimate friends who could, in those final days, have helped him swallow the bitter pill of truth, or just in some way accompany him. Until that moment his isolation had always seemed quite natural, something that happened to all men of a certain age and so couldn't be put down to his personality. I myself had no friend I'd want to see at my deathbed. But when I saw my father's happy, relaxed expression after a dose of morphine—his brow clear for the first time, the querulous twist of his lips finally erased—I understood that his lack of friends was, in fact, a personal defect; a stain on his character that possibly indicated some deeper turbulence; a fundamental blemish that I, as everything seemed to indicate, had inherited.

9

WHILE MY CLOTHES WERE DRYING IN THE SUN on the small clay-colored patio, Mariconchi switched on the TV and told me that I could watch whatever I wanted. She was going to prepare quesadillas for us both: "You must be starving, sweetie." I asked if she'd managed to get through to my father or sister, and she nodded before disappearing into the kitchen, from where, as if avoiding eye contact, she shouted, "Your daddy will be here in the early evening, sweetie. I'm going to take you to the airport so the two of you can get the next flight home."

All the TV channels had poor reception, except for one, which was showing a telenovela. I moved the rabbit-ear antenna around in vain and after a while switched the set off. On the telephone table, from where Mariconchi must surely have called my father, I found a small square message pad. I tore off one of the sheets and settled down to making an origami figure on the flowered dining room tablecloth, although I would have preferred a harder surface to obtain sharper creases. I only knew the basic folds by heart; for any animal I'd have needed to consult my instruction manual. But folding pieces of paper in half calmed me down, even when the activity had no actual end in view.

My great adventure was about to draw to a close, and it had been a failure. During the last fifteen hours, I'd become friends with Rat, one of the neighborhood celebrities; I'd made my debut as a smoker and had, for the first time, crossed over into forbidden territory, going beyond Taxqueña and Miramontes without the supervision of a responsible adult; I'd boarded a bus on my own, confronted a soldier with evil intentions, and now I was on a planet called Villahermosa, trying to do origami while the adoptive mother of my fantasies was preparing quesadillas. But all those incidents had served for nothing: I hadn't reached Chiapas, I hadn't found Teresa, and I hadn't sacrificed myself for her in the nascent revolution. And now my father had an excuse to punish me for the rest of my life: I'd never again see the sun or visit Guillermo's house after class.

I might even have to change schools, and instead of going back to Paideia in September, I'd be sent to a military academy, as I'd heard happened to uncontrollable children. In military school, all the staff would, of course, be like the adolescent soldier at the checkpoint on the highway, more interested in humiliating me and touching my legs than in teaching me how to do multiplication with decimal numbers or to memorize the history of the Mexican Revolution. My Choose Your Own Adventure books, my origami paper, and even my Zero Luminosity Capsule would be confiscated, and I'd be forced to sleep like a dog at the foot of my father's bed or sit in the living room with him, watching reruns of the Mexican team playing soccer until the 1998 World Cup in France came around.

In fact, there was no reason to assess the failure of my adventure in terms of the punishment that would be meted out to me. Not having reached Chiapas, not having found Teresa, not having become a hero in the eyes of my father, my sister, and her friends was its true measure. Reality had been too much for me. The world was vaster and more sinister than I'd imagined when I crossed Avenida Taxqueña, despite the presence of kindly figures like Mariconchi or less kindly ones like Rat. My failure consisted of having believed, in an arrogant, self-obsessed way, that growing up was a matter of undertaking grand projects and triumphing over adversity.

We ate the quesadillas in silence—I stoically tolerated the habanero chili sauce Mariconchi had added. Although I was still overexcited due to everything that had happened, weariness was beginning to get the better of me.

After eating, I lay on the couch while Mariconchi watched her telenovela. I didn't feel able to rest. Every time I began to nod off, something jolted me awake: an image or the sensation of falling, or the fear of missing something important. A few hours later Mariconchi touched my shoulder and told me I could put on my pants (it seemed to me that the strong Tabasco sun had left them not just bone dry but also paler). Then, in a matter of minutes, we were leaving for the airport.

THREE

1

MY FIFTH-GRADE SCHOOL NOTEBOOKS—I still keep one or two, together with other documents from my childhood, in a cardboard box under my bed—should have been covered in red, glossy paper, with my name and class written clearly on the front. Of course neither my father nor I remembered that until the last minute (seven in the evening on Sunday), and despite driving around all the stationery stores in south Mexico City, the best we could find was a roll of paper in a color described as "peach red" that, in the eyes of any boy, was without a shadow of doubt pink. After three frustrated attempts to cover one notebook himself, my father knocked on Mariana's door and passed the task on to her, promising as a reward to take her to Tower Records in Zona Rosa the following weekend to buy an album. As Mariana covered my notebooks in pink paper, I foresaw the awful effects that stupid color would have on my daily life.

The first tragic discovery of the academic year was that I'd been transferred to the B group of fifth grade because my father, overwhelmed by Teresa's disappearance and my later flight, had paid the school fees late, by which time my usual class was full. This meant that I was no longer able to sit next to Guillermo and, in spite of having already spent five years at Paideia, was forced to make a new group of friends, as if I'd just joined the school. Although I could still see my former companions during recess, it wouldn't be the same, since I'd have missed out on the classroom anecdotes that underlay the dynamics of the group.

The first days were disorienting. I couldn't shake off the sense of unreality that had taken hold of me since the journey to Villahermosa. A rumor was going around the school—I guess it must have been started by some friend Mariana had fallen out with—that our mother had joined the Zapatista uprising. Stories portraying my mom as an international terrorist, an underground heroine, or a downright liar spread around the schoolyard and among the groups of children waiting for their parents when class had finished for the day. The most outlandish versions of the legend attributed several killings to Teresa and promoted her to leadership of a rebel army.

The presidential elections had taken place just before the new school year, and a sort of political frenzy took hold of the children, who openly declared their affiliation to either PRD or PAN and were unhappy about the victory of the PRI candidate, Ernesto Zedillo. In a middle-class, progressive school like Paideia, the majority of the pupils tended to repeat the social-democratic opinions of their parents and teachers. And that was why the preponderant theory was that the defeat of the Left could be blamed on the Zapatistas, who hadn't backed the PRD candidate, Cuauhtémoc Cárdenas, and had formed a distraction with all their "fuss in the jungle," as the civics teacher had called the National Democratic Convention that had taken such a powerful hold on Teresa's political imagination.

At first none of my new classmates had the courage to ask directly about my mother, but the veiled allusions and smirks—eager to humiliate and greedy for gossip—were eloquent enough to make it clear that my social life was going to be fucked up for quite a while. To top it all, my best friend from previous years, the peerless Guillermo, decided that any association with me would have negative consequences for his public image.

"Cut," in school jargon, was a magic phrase, expressed by the symbolic act of making a circle with the thumb and forefinger and then dramatically separating them in the face of another child; from that moment, diplomatic relations between the two children were broken off and could only be restored, after mutual consensus, by means of the reverse symbolic act, termed "paste." Guillermo gave me the cut one recess in the first week of class and, as if by contagion, the gesture spread through the other children, my former playmates, during the following days until I was left isolated. This adept maneuver placed Guillermo at the peak of his popularity, making him the indisputable leader of both fifth-grade groups, while I was relegated to the marginality of a pariah, alongside Rodolfo Casillas, the caretaker's son (discriminated against on grounds of class) and Viridiana Lombardo, a girl from Guadalajara, newly arrived in the capital, whose accent and regional idioms made her an easy target. That is to say, as usual, the whiplash of childhood orthodoxy fell on those in any way different, and my status as "son of a guerrillera," as I began to be called by some, located me on the side of the oppressed.

What I found hardest about my lack of school friends was having no one to tell about the things that had happened to me during the vacation. In the safety of my Zero Luminosity Capsule, I'd fabricated a version of the story (excluding the episode of the briefs abandoned in the filthy toilet) that, I calculated, would even impress the most cynical and abusive of the sixth-grade children.

Now, during recess, I wandered from one side of the playground to the other, hoping against hope that someone would ask me what I'd done during the previous months so that I could show my true worth. But no one ever asked, and when I tried to buddy up with Rodolfo Casillas and timidly broach the topic of vacation, he told me that he'd spent his helping his father to make a piece of furniture, and then walked off before I could say anything.

Things weren't any better inside the classroom. Until then, if not an exemplary student, I'd at least been consistent. I compensated for my innate inability to do math with long hours of study at home under Teresa's cold gaze, and with top marks in history and language. Without my mother there to make me do my homework, and with the added emotional stress of having no friends, my attention span plunged drastically, and I came close to failing the diagnostic test we were given at the beginning of each year. As a consequence, my father grounded me in the evenings, which meant that my hopes of meeting Rat and telling him the whole of my Tabascan odyssey were also frustrated.

In that pitiful scenario, confined to my punishment-room, without the will to open fresh investigations into Teresa's whereabouts and activities, I turned again to origami.

I found it boring. Not only were the paper animals that resulted from all my efforts still unrecognizable, but the very activity of folding pieces of paper in two had lost all meaning. Suddenly, it felt like a childish whim that had engrossed me in some very remote past. I wondered how I could possibly have spent so many hours on such a silly pastime, angry at myself or at that version of myself that had ceased to exist at some point between Taxqueña and Villahermosa.

Perhaps in reaction to my origami period, as a sort of sequel to the exercise of folding leaves to extract the midrib from the ramifying veins, I began to create a general theory based on the differences between the two hemispheres. It suddenly seemed that everything I did with my left hand had a different, almost magical meaning. My right hand, reserved for the practical things of life (like doing homework), was a worldly extremity, while the left seemed to me to be invested with greater dignity. The expression "starting out on the wrong foot," with its implicit understanding that the wrong foot was the left, was a fallacy: everything that started out on the left foot had a stronger connection to the spiritual world, to the sacred, even.

And for precisely that reason, folding the leaves of bushes down the middle and making origami pagodas were impossible, fallacious activities: the hemispheres of reality were not, as in the Cartesian plane, equivalent or neutral, but charged with hidden attributes and meanings.

It's unlikely that I came up with that idea on my own. In those days, theories about the lateralization of brain functions had filtered through into many areas of popular culture, and it's possible that I'd seen reports on the TV about the functioning of the brain that particularly stimulated my imagination. I do remember overusing the word "hemisphere" in class, thus gaining a reputation for nerdiness and deepening the chasm of hatred that separated me from my fellow pupils. I guess I learned the term from the same program that suggested the basic principles of my rudimentary cosmology.

What happened was that I started to make conscious decisions about everything. At school, in the language class, I attempted to write an assignment on concrete and abstract nouns using my left hand. The result was a disaster: barely comprehensible squiggles like squashed spiders on the page. That experiment resulted in a severe reprimand from the teacher, who thought I was taking the piss, and then an awkward conversation with the school psychologist, who spent an hour trying to convince me that I'd written the assignment in a six-year-old's hand because I wanted to return to that point in my life. I made no response, neither confirming nor denying his theory, since I suspected that silence would be much less dangerous than explaining my idea of the superiority of the left hemisphere.

My experiments continued in PE class: I would start the hundred-meter sprint with my left foot, pass the basketball with my left hand, ask the teacher to let me play on the left wing during soccer games. As I'd always been useless at sports, no one noticed that I'd suddenly gotten a bit worse at everything, while my spiritual training, associated with the left hemisphere, benefited enormously.

My Zero Luminosity Capsule began to feel too small for me, as if I'd grown a few inches on the journey back from Villahermosa. Since my back began to hurt if I spent more than an hour in there, I gradually stopped using it.

I clearly recall the last time I entered the capsule. I was considering the necessity of developing my left biceps when I remembered an episode that seemed pertinent.

When I was seven and a half, my father had the tiny interior garden of our house in Educación cemented over. To call it a garden was an exaggeration: it was, in fact, a narrow rectangular strip of grass of no more than six feet by fifteen. A line was strung from one end to the other, and that was where Teresa hung the laundry out to dry. While Kurt—my sister's red-eared terrapin—was still alive, that rectangular garden was, in addition, his domain: he used to roam through the weeds in the mornings, peacefully chewing on the pieces of papaya we left for him on a saucer.

I don't know why my father decided that small garden had to be covered over. It possibly annoyed him that insects sometimes got into the living room through the sliding doors, and he thought putting down cement would get rid of them; or perhaps the cement was more in line with the notions of progress and sophistication that seemed to rule his life and ambitions than yellowing grass. The point is that he decided to overlay that minuscule nature reserve with cement. Mariana complained bitterly and took the terrapin to her bedroom, where it lived a year or two longer until one unhappy morning it expired after eating a piece of carpet.

A friendly builder with an amusing turn of phrase spent four days converting the garden into a patio. When the work was finished, and all that was left was for the cement to dry, Teresa suggested something I thought was fantastic fun: I was to be allowed to leave my handprint in the wet cement. Beside the handprint, she would use a stick to write the date so that, as time passed, it would be possible to compare the size of my hand with that print. Mariana was also invited to participate in the activity, but she declared that it was the kind of dumb stuff little kids did and went to her room to play with the exiled Kurt.

During the first months, I compared the size of my hand with the print in the cement on a daily basis, hoping to see if it had grown overnight.

But my interest gradually waned and my handprint was lost to oblivion, only stepped on by Teresa when she was pinning up the laundry.

Uncomfortably squeezed into my Zero Luminosity Capsule, I also recalled that, while the work was going on, my father constantly referred to the cement as "concrete": "How's the concrete looking?" he'd ask with wearying insistence every couple of hours, to which the builder would reply in terse monosyllables.

At the age of seven and a half, I had a very vague notion of the word "concrete," but by ten I was in a position to understand the difference between concrete and abstract nouns, so it seemed evident that my hand was, in *concrete* terms, a fundamental aspect of my theory of hemispheres. If it turned out that the print was of my right hand—as I seemed to remember—then it was clear that dominion over the *concrete* things of this world corresponded to that hemisphere.

I exited the Zero Luminosity Capsule, proud of the complexity of my philosophy, and removed the pillows and the sign I'd placed inside the closet: the capsule was redundant, it had fulfilled its function in my life and the moment had come to move on.

I ran down to the small cement patio and measured my hand against the print. It was indeed of my right hand, and I'd now outgrown it.

After that discovery, my manias about left and right sides took on mystical overtones. I made a patch from an old T-shirt and got into the habit of covering my left eye while I was at school, as if I were reserving its use for more important things. It goes without saying that such actions not only contributed to my further marginalization, but also set off all the alarms among the teaching staff at Paideia, so I was told I had to see the psychologist every Friday while the other children were enjoying the lunch break.

Another thing that happened during those first weeks of class was that I wet the bed a couple of times. This abnormality, which I associated with the episode at the military checkpoint on the highway to Villahermosa, felt deeply shameful. Why now, when I'd grown up— my right hand, much larger than the print in the concrete, was proof of this—when I'd stopped making origami figures and was no longer afraid of the Bogeyman, why had I started wetting the bed again like a four-year-old? The embarrassment those episodes produced was so intense that I did my utmost to cover them up: I used to put a couple of T-shirts in my pajama bottoms so that if I did wet myself, the urine wouldn't seep through, stain the mattress, and give my secret away. In the mornings, I'd get into the shower with the damp T-shirts and wash out the urine in the stream of hot water before hiding them under my bed, which meant they took a long time to dry and continued to smell damp for days.

FROM AN EARLY AGE I HAD THE SENSE that my father's death wasn't going to be a particularly traumatic or depressing event. Having survived Teresa's demise, the extinction of my father seemed something inevitable, maybe slightly sad, but not capable of radically or irreversibly changing my life. I'd have loved to have been right on that point.

Some nights in the hospital, when I was alone, keeping watch over my father, I'd walk to one of the waiting rooms to read. I'd stay there with my book until dawn, then go back to the room and doze in the uncomfortable armchair until the nurse arrived to carry out her routine morning checks and give my father a bed bath.

Since I tended to be too tired to concentrate on anything dense or demanding, I decided to reread some of the titles that had made an impression on me in my childhood. Naturally, I wouldn't have had the patience to skim the pages of my Choose Your Own Adventure novels (wouldn't have even known where to find them), but I did feel the urge to return to other classics that had at some moment or other helped me to forget the systematic contempt my classmates displayed during my last two years at elementary school.

So, in the off-white light of the waiting room, I reread *The Call of the Wild* by Jack London, Stevenson's *Treasure Island,* and part of Jules Verne's *Twenty Thousand Leagues Under the Sea,* which I finally gave up on when I lost the necessary concentration. My eyes ached constantly and the neon lighting was intolerable. I tried listening to music or podcasts through headphones. I tried playing solitaire or losing myself in the more engrossing games on my cell phone, but sooner or later, I abandoned these activities in despair, and ended by spending the rest of the night doing nothing, staring fixedly at some corner of the waiting room.

It was in that state of idle stupefaction that a nurse found me in the early hours of May 6, 2015, when she came to tell me that my father's heart rate had fallen dramatically and that the nightshift intern was with him.

On my way back to the room, I stopped to glance in the mirrored glass covering a fire extinguisher. My face, traversed by the instruction

"Break in case of emergency," suddenly seemed very similar to my father's. The same bags under the eyes, the same forehead with its ever-receding hairline, the same crooked, bulbous nose. I can't have stood there for more than three or four seconds but, during that brief pause, I was certain that I was seeing myself as others saw me.

I'd spent years scrutinizing myself in the mirror in search of Teresa's features. During my adolescence I'd kept a careful watch on the changes in my face, hopeful that she would in some way manifest herself, that she would return to my life via the oblique route of DNA. The notion I had of my own features was conditioned by that wistful gaze, by that desire to incarnate Teresa. But all of a sudden, walking toward my father's death—and toward my own death—I was offered a momentary vision of my face in all its objective ugliness, in all its unhappiness. There was nothing of Teresa there, not even anything of myself: it was my father's face, stuck onto mine, like something in a bad sci-fi movie. Whatever I did, he would stay with me, breathing within my breath, walking in my footsteps. All that could be expected of the future was that, with the passing years, my face would increasingly resemble his until one day, in a hospital bed, my dying-man's features would be my father's, and his pain finally my pain. At that moment, all the hours I'd spent in denial would manifest themselves in my guts, their weight forcing me down to the center of the earth, forcing me down into the tomb.

3

ONE DAY, WHEN WE WERE JUST FINISHING DINNER, the telephone rang. Mariana ran to answer it in her bedroom, but was disappointed to find that the call was for me. I took it in the living room.

It was Guillermo. He was having a birthday party the following week and wanted to invite me. As the tone of his voice was stiffly formal and I could hear muttered words in the background, I deduced that his mother had made him call. I accepted the invitation and put down the phone.

That night, lying in the darkness of my room—not as dark as my former Zero Luminosity Capsule—I considered the possible reasons why Guillermo's mother would have forced him to make that call. There could be no doubt that the news of Teresa's disappearance had reached the grown-ups. The school psychologist was untiring in his efforts to get me to say something on the topic, although it was obvious that he didn't dare ask me outright. Maybe Guillermo's parents (who were vaguely acquainted with Teresa due to my friendship with their son) planned to interrogate me during the party. Maybe they were working with the police and intended to pump me for information that would lead to my mother's arrest. Or maybe—this was the most plausible explanation—they felt sorry for me, not just because my mother had, according to gossip, gone to the mountains of the southeast of Mexico to join the revolution but also because, overnight, Guillermo had decided that he hated me.

I tried not to get my hopes up about the party. My friend and his inner circle were still shunning me during recess. It wasn't just a matter of refusing to say a word to me: there was something arrogant and defiant in the way they ignored me. They used to make a point of passing close by, flaunting their camaraderie to stress my exclusion. They smiled maliciously or whispered among themselves when one of the school bullies gave me a loud slap during the flag-raising ceremony on Monday mornings or pushed me down the stairs on the way to class.

But despite all those indications to the contrary, hope continued to glimmer somewhere deep inside me: there was the chance that at the party, away from the school dynamic, their hearts would soften and they would once again include me in the group.

It wasn't so much that I needed to belong to the group: apart from the stories that formed a bond between Guillermo and myself, I didn't feel particularly attracted to that gang. But I needed a break. School had always been an oasis of normality, a refuge from the conflicts at home—the arguments between my father and Mariana, Teresa's dark mood after reading some article in the newspaper that sparked off fresh bouts of domestic tension. One of the unforeseen and most unpleasant consequences of her departure was that the separation between school and home had dissolved: their conflicts were now related, as if two worlds had suddenly collided, causing devastation in both.

At midday on Saturday my father drove me to Guillermo's house. On the way, I persuaded him to stop to choose a gift. After a few minutes of pleading I managed to talk him into buying the latest Super Nintendo cartridge. Teresa had never allowed us to have video games, but it was an open secret that when I went to visit Guillermo I'd spend three or four hours in front of the screen losing every game—with my friend alternating between glee and despair at being able to humiliate me for a whole afternoon—while their domestic employee fed us sandwiches, cookies, and the sort of junk food I'd never seen for sale in any store in my neighborhood.

A Super Nintendo game was a gift of such generosity that it bordered on the absurd: kids usually gave action figures or throwaway toys that would be broken by the end of the party. But none of that was enough for me: I had to purchase Guillermo's friendship, purchase my access to that group of popular boys, buy their silence about and forgiveness of my guerrillera mother.

Guillermo's house was much larger than ours and was located in a gated community. I'd slept over on a number of occasions during the past two years but still found its pomp imposing. My father's gold Tsuru was like an intruder in those streets, which were accustomed to much more luxurious vehicles. He must have realized this: he drove more slowly than usual, negotiating the speed bumps with extreme care, as if he were afraid of breaking them and being charged for the damage. Anyone watching us from the sidewalk might have thought that the car itself was aware of its shortcomings.

Guillermo's mother received me with a degree of warmth that felt suspicious. My father, intimidated by the financial superiority of the hosts, accepted a glass of water, which he drank standing up, visibly uncomfortable, before explaining that he had things to do and making a speedy exit. Guillermo's mother gave me a soda and said I could leave my gift on the table with the others, but I managed to sneak it with me into the garden, where some of the guests were already running around noisily. My idea was for Guillermo to open the present in front of all the boys and—won over by my largesse—immediately ask me to join in the general fun.

As I approached the group of five children playing in the garden, far from the protective eyes of Guillermo's mom, I knew that I'd made a mistake. My gift, enveloped in paper with a clown design, suddenly seemed ridiculous, and I began to wish that I'd left it on the table, as everyone else had done. Guillermo looked surprised to see me; perhaps he'd assumed that, in spite of the phone call, my common sense would prevail and I'd finally decide not to show my face. But after a momentary hesitation, he seemed to become aware of the possibilities my appearance offered in terms of his legitimation as a leader.

"What are you doing out here? Didn't Mom tell you that the girls are staying inside?" His words hurt me, but they also seemed senseless: there were no girls at the party.

His greeting made clear that it wasn't going to be an easy day.

My former friend grabbed the present from my hands and effortlessly tore open the clown gift wrapping. The other four or five boys looked on with expressions of malicious anticipation. I was indignant to find that among them were some of the dumb but popular boys Guillermo and I used to openly mock before that fatal summer vacation. His transformation was more complete than I'd supposed: not only had he turned his back on me, but also on the boy he'd been just a few months earlier.

Guillermo sneered, said he already had that game, and threw it into the undergrowth. That part of the garden had been let run wild, with huge banana plants and coffee bushes that created a jungle effect. "Beat it," he said, and then pushed me with both hands, causing me to momentarily lose my balance. "Or are you going to tell your whore of a mother to come and kill us?"

That new barb was more deeply hurtful than any of the earlier ones, not because of the insinuation that Teresa was a whore—an insult that had become hackneyed due to its ubiquitous use at school and in the neighborhood—but for the implication that she was a murderer; on Guillermo's lips, that accusation felt for the first time seriously beyond the pale.

I'd never, until that moment, considered the possibility that Teresa had killed anyone. Even if she'd joined the rebels in balaclavas, even if it turned out that she was living in a camp in the middle of a war zone, I was incapable of imagining her firing a gun or throwing a grenade. Her violence was of a different variety: it consisted of looking you in the eyes and coolly saying things that hurt: "I'm disappointed in you." Accusing my mom of being a killer was an unbearable lie, and the only possible response was to destroy the person who had pronounced that falsehood.

I had the element of surprise on my side: Guillermo wasn't expecting things to come to blows. But he was taller and stronger than me. I got in a first punch to his chest—spraining my wrist in the process—but in a matter of seconds, and with great ease, he overwhelmed me. Before I knew what was happening, I was on the ground, Guillermo's knee pressing on the middle of my back and his hand pushing my face into the damp grass. I thrashed about and unsuccessfully tried to roll over. I heard laughter behind me; not Guillermo's but the other boys'. One said something I didn't catch and there was a fresh burst of laughter. Then another boy, wearing a red T-shirt, decided to join in the humiliation. He came up and kicked my shin, close to the knee. "The little girl's going to wet herself," he said. Out of the corner of my eye I saw him opening his zipper and gesturing Guillermo to stand aside. Seeing what he had in mind, Guillermo got to his feet and put his foot on my neck so that I was still immobilized.

A stream of urine fell onto my pants, around my rump, splashing my T-shirt slightly. Then the warm dampness filtered through to my briefs, wetting my asshole and my shrunken testicles. The boys who had stood watching these proceedings continued to laugh or contributed to the herd response by whooping jubilantly.

It was only then that I stopped struggling, let myself go limp, closed my eyes, and savored the taste and texture of the earth beneath the grass. I could no longer hear the laughter. Silence pervaded everything around me, and for a moment I had the impression of being inside my Zero Luminosity Capsule, far from all the noise and lights of the world.

When I opened my eyes again, Guillermo and the others had gone. Sound returned and I made out their voices in the distance, playing soccer in another area of the large garden. I stood up, wiped my face, and brushed off the front of my T-shirt. My eyes were stinging, as if I were going to cry at any moment, but no tears came. My neck hurt and I had a pain in a bone in the center of my chest I'd never been aware of before. The smell of urine rose to my nose and I remembered my own urine, my own smell on the way to Villahermosa, when I'd torn the tag bearing my full name from my briefs. I noticed that I was wearing the same pants as I had on that day—the same pants Mariconchi had washed in her house in Villahermosa while I was taking a shower—this time stained with urine that wasn't mine.

I put my hand in my right pocket, and there it was: the fabric tag bearing my full name, reminding me that it would always be the same, that those two surnames would stalk me to the end of my days: son of my father and son of my mother, in that order.

At that instant I'd have given anything to be Úlrich González.

Guillermo's mom didn't ask what had happened. She seemed disgusted to see me in her living room stinking of piss. There was another woman with her; they were drinking coffee and eating cookies. The host apologized to her guest and forcefully grasped my wrist. She dragged me upstairs and left me standing in the hallway. "Don't move an inch, you'll get everything dirty," she said and went into a room, closing the door behind her. I heard her speaking to my sister on the phone. My father hadn't even had time to return home. Guillermo's mom was extremely anxious to get me out of the house before any other guest could see the state I was in. She told my sister that she wanted to protect me from the children, who would give me a hard time if they found out about what she termed my "accident." I didn't have the courage to tell her that her son and his friends were a bunch of shits.

She finally agreed to send me home in a cab, with a driver who acted as the family's ad hoc chauffeur. Guillermo's mom lent me a pair of her son's old pants and put mine in a grocery bag that, to my extreme embarrassment, I had to carry with me.

During the whole journey home, I stared through the window of the cab. My rage had abated and I was left with a profound sense of sadness. Mexico City seemed grayer, more fractured, dirtier than usual. At a traffic signal, a fire-eater asked for money and the cab driver rolled up the window without even responding to the request.

4

A FEW YEARS AGO I READ AN ARTICLE in a specialist magazine about memory function. I've never been a big consumer of popular science, but for days afterward I was left thinking about the findings of that particular study. The subheading was eye-catching and grandiloquent: "Every time you remember something that happened in the past, your brain distorts it." This conclusion had been drawn by a group of neurologists in an English university who had charted the nerve impulses of a large sample of people.

The authors explained how the memories we return to most frequently are the most inaccurate, the least faithful to reality. When we recall a specific event, what we often remember is the experience of having remembered it before, not the original event. So, every time we remember a scene, that scene has a more tenuous relationship to the lived experience. Details are added, certain colors intensified, interpretation is superimposed on fact. Of course, in the article, this had a neurological explanation that I've forgotten, and all I have now is the metaphor.

Remembrance is destructive. Not just in terms of the memory, as the neurologists claim in that article, but also for the subject who remembers— I'm adding that part. The memory and the subject wipe each other out in the exercise of remembering, until the memory becomes an invention and the subject is more alone than before, because the thing recalled no longer exists, is just a replica of a replica of a replica.

The day my father died is irretrievable, lost in some tangle of neural circuitry that I'll never be able to access. What I'm left with is a replica of a replica that says this: my father lost consciousness at around one in the morning. I rang Mariana to let her know, but the answering machine cut in, so I left a message. I sat on a stool by his hospital bed and began to talk to my father. Although I was initially hesitant—embarrassed in case the nursing staff should overhear or anyone should see me—my words eventually began to come more easily. By about half past three I was speaking fluently, only occasionally lapsing into silence for a few minutes at a time.

I spoke to him about the past: told him about the time Teresa fainted outside the market and when I kicked a pigeon. I told him that when I was ten, Rat had accompanied me to the Taxqueña bus station, and also that I'd seen Rat again, a few weeks before, having an argument with his teenage daughter not far from the hospital. I told my unconscious father about the restroom in the service station on the way to Villahermosa, where I'd left behind my briefs, and about the bathroom in Mariconchi's house.

I also used those hours to communicate certain focuses of resentment that had been smoldering in my chest for some time. I reproached him for his narrow-mindedness, the way he'd distanced Mariana, his violent rages, his need to control everyone around him. I'd never have dared to say any of that if he could hear me. Unlike my sister, who'd been openly challenging his authority from the age of fifteen, I'd borne my father's abuse in absolute silence. When my patience was reaching its limits, I'd try to tell myself that Teresa's death had been as painful for him as it had for us, even more so, because he'd known her longer.

At four in the morning my father briefly recovered consciousness and muttered something I couldn't make out due to the tubes connecting him to life. Whatever it was, they were his last words. I'm not sure why, but I'm convinced they weren't important.

Three or four times during the following forty minutes I believed he was dead and called the nurse, who felt his pulse and shook her head, looking me straight in the face without compassion or ceremony. Finally, at seventeen minutes past five, he did die. When his decease had been confirmed, I held his hand for a moment, as a sort of farewell, and then left the room, following the doctor.

Mariana arrived just before six. I've no idea if she was sorry to have missed that final moment. The truth is, I guess, that she'd said her good-byes long ago.

Neither of us cried. We'd had time to assimilate, even desire, the death of the man who had, to a great extent—against his will, against ours— brought us up.

My father's will stated that the vigil was to be held in a funeral home; a gray, airless place that offered substantial discounts to the staff of the bank where he'd worked.

Someone had left a yellow bucket containing a dirty rag in one corner of the room where the coffin stood. At some point I thought of asking for it to be removed, but then told myself that it wasn't worth the effort. My father's former colleagues and their wives must have had the same thought. His boss of the previous ten years, a man his own age, told me a few of the anecdotes about my father that everyone always remembered: the time he bought a cake for his secretary, convinced—wrongly—that it was her birthday; another occasion when he'd accidentally made a pun on a client's name; and yet another when it had taken three or four of them to prevent him from punching someone in a cantina. They were silly stories that portrayed him as a simple, bad-tempered, but to some extent likeable man.

Mariana had a hard time masking her disdain of those people. She shook hands, smiled occasionally, and then went outside to smoke, taking Katia or one of her female friends with her. For my part, I hadn't invited anyone; I'd felt no need for moral support. It was all the same to me if I had to spend the night in the company of account executives, area managers, and second cousins.

A week after the funeral, Mariana and I had a meeting with the lawyer. Victor Garmendia was one of the few of my father's acquaintances who neither worked at the bank nor were members of the club. I've never understood how they got to know each other, and he was never invited to our house, but my father used to refer to Garmendia with a degree of warmth that was rare in him.

On meeting the lawyer in the flesh, however, I had the impression that the feeling wasn't mutual: he spoke of my father as a long-standing client with whom he'd had the occasional beer, but little else.

We agreed that Garmendia would take charge of the sale of the house in Educación—in exchange for a percentage of the purchase price—as soon as we handed over the keys. My task was to clear out the house: to sell or give away everything it contained. Mariana preferred not to be involved.

I'd left my job teaching Spanish as a foreign language to be with my father during the last months of his life. It was a badly paid job that had involved tolerating intolerably spoiled gringo students. The truth is, I'd been looking for an excuse to pack it in for ages.

Without the income from my classes, and given the need to empty the house in Educación, I felt that the most sensible course of action would be to move in there for a few days, and so also save the long daily commute from the apartment I was then renting in Santa María la Ribera.

Before I'd even gotten the door fully open, the smell hit me with the clarity, the physical reality, of an image. It was difficult to believe that the house in Educación could still smell exactly the same in spite of the fact that it was now uninhabited, that my father was dead, that Teresa was dead, that Mariana hadn't lived there for years, and that I myself, to the extent that time allowed such stunts, was a different person from the one who had once dwelled between those walls.

I dumped my backpack in my old bedroom and contemplated the titanic task that lay before me. Nothing seemed to have changed since the time I lived there. My father had hardly moved anything in the house, as if he'd been holding his breath for years, fearing to the last any trace of change.

I decided to organize the contents of the house into three broad categories: things to be sold, things to be given away, and things I'd prefer to talk to Mariana about before taking any action.

I began in the living room, where everything was saleable: the couch with its ineradicable stains, the ten volumes of the *Encyclopedia of Mexico*, a box of movies on VHS. The only thing my father had updated was the television set: I could probably get a good price for that immense, brand-new flat-screen.

After quickly sorting out the living room, I decided to move on to the kitchen, postponing the inspection of my former bedroom for a moment of greater spiritual equanimity. My father's room would come last: the mere sight of its drawn-curtain half-light caused my breathing to accelerate.

That first night I was unable to sleep. My old bed was too short and the dust I'd disturbed in the living room had floated through the whole house, causing me an allergic reaction. Standing at my bedroom window, I watched the sun rise over Educación.

On the second day of the clear-out I went to get something to eat at a nearby street market and, among the food stands, saw an old pickup truck with flaking paint and a banner reading, "Furniture, clothing, and trinkets bought." It seemed as good an option as any. When I approached the window of the pickup, I found the vehicle was empty. I looked around and inquired at a fruit stand, where I was told that the "junkman" would be back shortly. I leaned up against the dilapidated bodywork of the truck to wait in the sunlight.

After a few minutes, I felt a hand on my shoulder and turned to find myself face-to-face with Rat. He was the same older man who had appeared a few weeks before in the vicinity of the hospital. This time he was alone, without the teenage girl I'd seen him arguing with in the street.

Rat didn't appear surprised to see me, but neither did he give the least sign of recognition. "What can I do for you?" he asked. He had the raspy voice of a chain-smoker of unfiltered Delicados. "Don't you remember me? I'm Mariana's brother . . . No. 23, Calle H." Rat made a vague gesture, as if saying that he couldn't care less about the past, as if the fact of our having met twice—after twenty years during which we'd scarcely heard word of each other—just before and just after my father's death, had no importance. "And what can I do for you, Mariana's brother from Calle H?" he asked in a sarcastic tone, making his indifference clear. I gave up the attempt to be friendly. Maybe I was the only person who cared about the summer of '94. Nobody, not Mariana, Rat, or anybody else, seemed interested in reviving the story. "My father died not long ago, and I'm clearing out his house. There are a lot of things I could sell you."

Rat didn't offer his condolences or show the least contrition. He told me that he'd swing by later to check how much there was, if it would fit in his pickup, and how many trips he'd need to make. He gave me his card: "'Rat,' Dealer in Antique Furniture," it said; below was a drawing of a giant rat in dark glasses, driving a moving van. We shook on it; Rat's hand was rough, callused, hard as concrete.

On the way back to the house I bought two cans of beer and a disposable dust mask. Drinking the beer, surrounded by the cardboard boxes scattered around the living room, I wondered where Rat would take all that stuff. He probably had a partner who would resell it all. It pleased me to think that there was a place in La Lagunilla or the antique market in Portales that would display all the material goods that had filled my father's life: trophies of an existence dedicated to the accumulation of hand tools. Someone would stop one Saturday to ask the price of a monkey wrench and around him, solemnly silent, would be what remained of my father, his pillaged mausoleum of junk. There was some form of poetic justice in the fact that Rat was to take on the task. As if, in spite of his reticence and unnatural aloofness, he were doomed to accompany me, one more time, on that rocky transition out of Colonia Educación.

I don't consider myself to be particularly attached to material goods. Throwing out the dreadful seascape that had adorned the hallway during my whole childhood didn't involve the least sacrifice. And it was just as easy to get rid of the electric appliances and the ornaments that had populated the shelves of my youth. I even began to think that the clear-out was going to be a relatively simple process, that in a matter of days I'd have disposed—without consequences or regrets—of a past that had been weighing me down for so long.

That afternoon, I finished in the kitchen, and in a burst of energy also classified everything in Mariana's former bedroom, now converted into a junk room. Rat turned up later, at about eight o'clock, and cast a professional eye over the collection of boxes in the living room and kitchen. I told him that there was more stuff upstairs, but he decided that it wasn't necessary to look it over: he already had an idea of what he'd need for the job.

The following morning I went to the market in search of more cardboard boxes, and within a couple of hours had decided on the fate of everything in my bedroom. I set aside a few of my elementary school notebooks, two or three novels, and some CDs from my teenage years that had nostalgia value. Everything else could be sold.

To cut a long story short, the clear-out progressed without incident until I got to my father's bedroom: the room that had once also been Teresa's. There was the bed that my mother had slept in until that Tuesday in July or August 1994; the desk in the corner at which she'd most likely written the farewell letter to my father; the night table on which I'd found that letter under a ridiculous porcelain dog.

For me, there was a touch of the museum about that room. In some way it resembled one of those houses of historical personages, preserved intact for the delight of tourists. Except that there, I was able to become a tourist of my own history. Since it was the area of the house I'd entered least frequently during all those years, for me it preserved more clearly than any other the memory or ghost of my mother: I could imagine Teresa reading, arguing, getting dressed in that room, suspended in a time before everything happened, like a hologram projected by my grief and fatigue.

5

ON SEPTEMBER 23, 1994, six days after the incident at Guillermo's party, my father said he needed to talk to us. Mariana and I were just coming in from school, and we were surprised to find him in the house at a time when he still should have been at the bank. His hair was tousled and he hadn't shaved; he was wearing his Sunday pants. The atmosphere had been exceptionally tense for the whole of that week.

I'd taken it for granted that he was annoyed with me because of the party, but had no idea how to scold me since the whole situation was so odd: a child of almost eleven wetting himself at a party inspired more pity than rage, and my father tended to have a very hard time dealing with complex emotions.

At school, the regime of jibes and humiliations to which I'd been subjected continued, although never reaching the nadir of the party. Retreating behind a planter during recess, sitting with my knees drawn up and my glossy-pink-paper covered notebook open at the back pages, I passed the time writing my Left Hemisphere Theory as a means of evasion and philosophical consolation. I filled several of those pages in my spidery handwriting, explaining the magical associations of the left side, and the merely practical ("concrete," I wrote) ones assigned to the right.

One night, Mariana was unusually considerate. She entered my room without knocking and, with a sigh, lay down on my bed. Staring at the ceiling, she murmured, almost to herself: "I know things are really weird right now, shorty. But you'll see: my mom will come home soon and everything will sort itself out. They'll probably get divorced, but that's no big deal, all my friends' parents are divorced." And without waiting for any response, she went back to her bedroom and shut the door.

I'm now uncertain what I was thinking about Teresa in those days. I wasn't particularly interested in making conjectures about her life as an outlaw in the jungle, and although at times my imagination took flight to that region, in general I tried to keep my mind on any other subject. Most likely I was tired of so much change, so much asymmetry.

My father's tone presaged a serious conversation. Mariana was trying to pretend that she hadn't heard, like when she was asked to wash the dishes or come back early from Citlali's house. I didn't have the self-assurance to feign indifference: I sat in the living room, next to my father, in victim mode, ready to receive a sermon that, if things went badly, might degenerate into shouts and insults—as they generally did. Yet despite his unkempt appearance and the announcement that he had something to say to us, my father looked relatively calm.

"There's been an accident," he began, but then seemed lost for words and, after a momentary hesitation, had to start again, this time expressing himself more clearly. "Your mom was involved in an accident. A traffic accident. Teresa is dead."

I don't recall the rest of the conversation. But I do remember that the name Teresa sounded strange on his lips: for some reason I clung to that observation, as if trying to erase the real content of his message.

Mariana shouted some question or other and then—in a scream that degenerated into a wail—sobbed, "It's all your fault." She ran upstairs and slammed her bedroom door. That noise unblocked something inside me and I started to cry as I'd never cried before. It was a silent, muffled bout of tears, with spasms but no sound, like a mime. My father tried to hug me and I squirmed, contorting my body in an attempt to avoid his touch until I slid from the couch to the floor.

Later that evening, Mariana came out of her room with red eyes and the three of us sat together again in the living room. My father started to reassure us that everything was going to be fine, but realized how stupid that sounded and turned to more practical matters, which he was much better at. He announced that we'd have to stay in the house alone for a couple of days, while he went to Chiapas "to bring her back." In hindsight, the idea of leaving us alone after imparting such news seems eloquent proof not only of my father's profound ignorance of childrearing but, more importantly, his lack of empathy. But at that moment both my sister and I were in shock; neither of us knew what to say.

Mariana asked if Teresa had died in the war and he said she hadn't, that apparently she'd been living in downtown San Cristóbal and her brakes had failed on a nearby highway.

My eyelids suddenly began to droop, as if my whole body was asking for a respite after the awful news, and at some point I fell asleep on the couch. My father and Mariana also slept in the living room that night, if they did in fact sleep at all.

6

MARIANA CALLED MY CELL PHONE just when I was starting to clear my father's room—Teresa's room, because, for me, it had never stopped being hers. While we were talking I walked into the bedroom where my sister had spent so many hours listening to music, and then into mine, where I'd spent so much time folding sheets of paper or drafting theories.

She wanted to know how much longer it would take to empty the house, as there was a potential buyer interested in viewing it. This news annoyed me: it hadn't even been two weeks since the meeting and Garmendia had already found someone.

My sister wanted to dispose of the house as soon as possible so that she could put her share of the sale price to use. I could understand her urgency, had even come to share it, but once I was installed in the house, surrounded by boxes, piles of paper, and clothes, the idea of passing some time there, as a sort of personal farewell to my past, had begun to grow on me. Once the house in Educación was sold, Teresa would have finally departed, and my father too. The spaces in which they had loved, in which they had fought, and where they had watched us growing up would belong to other people. There was every possibility that the new owners would knock down a wall or completely remodel the whole house.

The single mattress on my old bed was now lying on the dusty floor. Rat had come by the day before, accompanied by a man to help with the heavy work, and had taken a good part of the furniture. While they were coming in and out of the house, I stood by the doorway, leaning against the wall, just as Teresa used to do when she was smoking. Rat and his assistant passed me carrying furniture, which they loaded into the pickup. My former Zero Luminosity Capsule was among those items.

At some point, Rat asked me if I wanted him to remove the stuff from Teresa's room as well. For a second I was tempted to say yes, that he could take everything before I'd even had time to look through it. Perhaps that would have been better: to close my eyes at the right moment. But common sense deserted me, and I said no, that I hadn't had time to check that room yet, but he could come back the following day.

"And what about the big bed in there?" he asked. He was referring, of course, to my father's bed; Teresa's bed. He was also referring to the double bed from which I'm now writing, in which I've spent a good part of my time over the last two years. "No. I'll hang on to that," I told him.

While Rat was tethering the precarious pile of large items of furniture onto the pickup, I thought that the living room, where he'd consumed beer and pizza and unsuccessfully courted Mariana during the summer of '94, must have sparked some memory in him. Maybe the speed with which Rat loaded everything onto the pickup had to do with an incipient sense of remorse, the early signs of a guilty conscience or at least of nostalgia: a tacit acceptance that the past had weight and meaning—that a walk to Taxqueña two decades before had, in some way, seeped through to his inner core too.

When he held out the roll of bills in payment for the goods, I looked into his eyes for some echo of that other moment: his hand—less callused in those days—holding out a few crumpled bills in the Autobuses del Sur terminal, before he abandoned me to my fate. But Rat looked away and drove off in his vehicle, leaving behind a trail of black exhaust fumes.

The floor of my former—now unfurnished—bedroom was littered with a variety of objects and papers that would have to be thrown out when the garbage truck came by. Before mustering the energy to check my parents' bedroom, I sat there for a moment, among the remaining rubble of my childhood.

At the other side of the room, on top of my old elementary school notebooks, I spotted an attempt at an origami frog. In comparison with all my other mediocre efforts, that frog wasn't too bad. I thought I'd eliminated all traces of my hobby with the move from childhood to adolescence, but I'd apparently overlooked the frog, which had survived two decades of oblivion with admirable dignity. It wasn't one of the figures I'd made from the colored paper that came with the manual Teresa had given me, but a white frog, constructed from the ruled page of a school notebook. I picked it up to take a closer look. The paper was stained around the folds, and I deduced that my hands had been dirty when I'd made them, or that I'd licked them into place.

Sitting by the window (the same window through which I'd so often feared to see the legendary Bogeyman climb), I meticulously unfolded the origami frog, trying as I did to remember the exact procedure I'd used to construct it. What had I been thinking about when I made that figure? More importantly, who had I been when I made it? Was there any relationship between that ten-year-old boy and the orphaned man of thirty-one now taking the figure apart?

The unfolded paper in my hands had an oracular aura. Written in pencil in spidery handwriting, three words in the center of the sheet were attempting to respond to all my questions: "the left side."

It was there in that room, a couple of years ago, a week after my father's death, that I remembered the extent of my hemispheric obsession: the evenings I'd spent practicing writing with my left hand; the patch I'd worn over my left eye for weeks; the hopeless attempts to chew on one side of my mouth that had kept me sitting at the dining room table long after my father and Mariana had left, when the afternoon sky had slipped into night with the impossible spectrum of colors produced by environmental pollution at sunset.

I felt something approaching pity for that boy who compensated for a painful, incomprehensible situation by adopting strange behaviors. That frog must have been one of the last I made before giving up origami. It was the product of a turbulent, unstable period when I was struggling to give some meaning, any meaning, to the news that Teresa, my mother, had died the most dreary of deaths on a secondary road, far from the jungle and revolution.

7

I DON'T REMEMBER HOW MANY DAYS MARIANA AND I SPENT alone in the house while my father was in Chiapas. Nor do I remember exactly what happened during those days. As if the news of Teresa's death had been a bomb that had gone off too close, I was dazed for a time, with a constant high-pitched whistling in my ears that just wouldn't go away.

I do know that Mariana never invited her girlfriends to come around during those days. We both slept in the living room and hardly ever went to any other part of the house, as though the whole upstairs area had a curse on it.

As a sedative, we left the television permanently switched on, although we did at times turn down the volume to sleep for a while: Mariana on the floor, wrapped in a blanket, I on the couch.

I know that I threw up the first day and then later had diarrhea. Mariana, more maternal than she had ever been in the past, made me many cups of chamomile tea. I remember that her face was swollen and she had a smear of dried snot on her cheek that she never washed off. I also remember that we watched violent cartoons—the sort Teresa used to ban—Mexican movies from the fifties, and an American soap opera that my sister liked. I have no idea what we ate or whether my father ever called us. I don't know if anyone rang the doorbell, and neither do I recall the sun coming up or setting. It was a continual night, longer than the long night on the bus to Villahermosa.

My father returned from Chiapas, bringing with him Teresa's ashes in a dark container that looked to me like a vase with a lid. Mariana went into a flying rage when she discovered that our mother had been cremated far away, with no other ceremony than the fire of the blast furnace reflected in my father's pupils. She screamed, cried, threatened to leave home and never come back. (That outburst would be reenacted, in almost identical form, during the following two years, until she turned eighteen and finally carried out her threat.)

My reaction was also negative, but more from a desire to imitate my sister than any personal stance. To tell the truth, I didn't understand what was going on, and wouldn't have even known how to behave if my father had turned up with Teresa's body in a coffin instead of that vase filled with ashes. The rite of saying one's last farewells to the mortal remains of a person was beyond my understanding, and to a great extent still is. If I hadn't managed to say good-bye properly that Tuesday in July or August when Teresa had left me in my sister's care, I wasn't going to do it then either.

I was allowed a few days off school and, during that time, my father's unprecedented attempts to show affection were more disturbing than comforting. If he saw me sitting on the couch in the living room, he'd put his arms around me and stay fixed in that position for a while, tense and silent, as if he'd forgotten the meaning of the gesture mid-embrace.

I had trouble sleeping. There were nightmares in which Guillermo and his group stole the vase containing Teresa's ashes and played soccer with it in the playground until it broke. When I woke up, I'd sit on my bed and do a series of exercises that involved only the left side of my body: I'd try to touch my shoulder blade with my left hand, turn my eyes to the left until they hurt: anything related to the left side. That personal liturgy succeeded in calming me a little, and even though I never slept through the whole night, I did at least rest for a while.

One night, however, the hemispheric exercises didn't work and I decided to go to the kitchen for a glass of water. As I was silently descending the stairs, I caught sight of my father sitting at the dining room table with a glass of tequila before him. He didn't see me, so I squatted down on the turn of the stairs and spied on him for a moment. Although I was viewing him from above, through the rails of the bannister, I was able to see his face. His expression was hard to read; it was as if he were attempting to solve some complex math problem or memorize a sequence of numbers. He was staring at a point on the tablecloth but, after a while, moved his eyes to focus on another spot. Every so often he took a sip from his shot glass, barely wetting his lips. What could he be thinking about? Was he blaming himself for Teresa's death? Was he sad, worrying about taking responsibility for us on his own? I considered going to him, putting my arms around him, and telling him that it wasn't his fault, that it had been an accident or fate. But just when I was about to offer consolation, his facial muscles relaxed. Where previously there had been incomprehension and emptiness, now, at first timidly, a smile was appearing. I'd never seen my father smile that way. It's most probably, I thought, a smile he wears when he's alone, when he thinks no one can see him. The smile grew broader. The crow's-feet around his eyes deepened. Then he began to laugh, silently; as if repressing the sound.

Squatting there, spying on my father, I recognized for the first time the similarity between that laugh and the one given by the soldier who had frisked me one night on the highway to Villahermosa. I slowly rose to my feet and silently went back up the stairs to my bedroom.

Twenty-one years went by without me thinking about that laugh. Or maybe it would be better to say that twenty-one years went by with me trying not to think about it, but the memory finally resurfaced, and the fact that I now live in solitary confinement, that I spend the greater part of my life lying on the left side of this bed, has, in some sinister, obscure way, to do with the persistence of that laugh in my memory.

8

I FOUND THE FOLDER IN ONE OF THE DESK DRAWERS. Perhaps sub-consciously anticipating the catastrophe, I'd put that drawer off until last. Once those papers were in order, I'd be able to say I'd finished with the room, the most difficult of all. Then all that would be left was to organize the removal of my parents' bed and the few other pieces of furniture that I'd decided to keep. In three or four days, I'd be able to hand over the keys to Garmendia.

It was a red, A4 Kraft folder. My first guess was that it would contain documents related to the insurance policy (true to his practical nature, before his death my father had said that they were in the desk), but as soon as I opened it, I realized that this was not the case. I immediately recognized the writing: Teresa's formal, elongated hand. The first sheet of paper I extracted from the folder was the letter I'd attempted to steal from my father's night table when I was ten.

After Teresa's death, I'd forgotten about the letter, or perhaps it no longer seemed important: the mystery was solved. According to my father, who had drip-fed us the story over the intervening years, Teresa went to La Realidad, Chiapas State, to attend the National Democratic Convention in the Lacandon jungle, convened by the Zapatista National Liberation Army. Politicians, intellectuals, journalists, academics, and international observers had also been present.

During that week, Teresa had listened to speeches made by the most important figures of the rebellion, and at mealtimes had debated with volunteers and students from different regions of the country. When the convention broke up she considered staying there, perhaps also join-ing the rebel ranks or becoming a volunteer in one of the communities, but someone told her that she couldn't, that she had to return to Mexico City, where she would be more useful raising funds and circulating true information. Disappointed, Teresa had decided to rent a small apart-ment on the outskirts of San Cristóbal. Her plans—again, according to my father—were not completely clear, but she was probably thinking of spending a couple of months there alone, taking a vacation from the family before returning to her life as a diligent housewife in Educación.

At heart, I always knew that it was a lie, an illusion created by my father, who wanted to convince himself (and us) that Teresa had always intended to come back. I never knew if he believed his own story or simply maintained it before us, but the truth is, I never made the effort to contradict him.

Teresa's letter didn't specify a precise plan, but she was resolute: she was going to Chiapas because she could no longer bear living with my father and knew that the indigenous peoples of Chiapas had "a lesson in dignity" to offer her.

Sitting at the desk, reading the letter, the red folder on my knees, I had the impression that the Teresa who had written those lines was very young. Until that moment I'd always imagined my mother to be a full-fledged adult, conscious of the weight of all her decisions, a person as rational and restrained as her robotic voice. But Teresa had also been a passionate woman beset by contradictory impulses. Her farewell letter allowed a vision of that aspect of her personality. There was a high ideological tone that, with the distance of time, I found slightly embarrassing. That letter seemed to have been written in a more heroic age; not in the final decade of the twentieth century, but much earlier, in the golden years of the student movement of the seventies, or at the dawn of the Cuban Revolution. Teresa employed terms like "alienation" and "capitalism" to complain about the oppression my father—undoubtedly—exercised over her; she used words like "struggle" and "victory" to define her own future.

It was a short letter, two sides of a piece of writing paper. The final paragraph was about us (Mariana and I). She asked my father, if he had an ounce of shame left in him, not to tell us lies about her. She couldn't ask him to explain her decision to us because she knew he wouldn't understand it himself, but she begged him not to set us against her. She promised to call from time to time and didn't rule out visiting us at some point, when her underground existence allowed.

It was very strange to read the same letter I'd furtively held in my hands for a moment twenty-one years before. Would I have understood anything if I'd read it all the way through then? Would I—as did in fact happen—have set out on a bus to follow Teresa through the southeast of Mexico if I'd known its content?

Those lines revealed something about my father I found painful to consider at that moment, when his body had only recently been interred. I'd always been aware that the relationship between him and Teresa was tense, and only very rarely fantasized about the possibility of them being really in love, but the letter showed a much higher level of tension, a sense of asphyxiation in Teresa that I'd never, at the age of ten, been able to read in her neutral voice and undemonstrative manner.

In the same red folder, underneath that letter, were—in the washed-out hues of early eighties photography—four color photographs. In the first, Teresa was standing beside a child of no more than three, who must have been Mariana. She was holding up a placard with the words "Free Nicaragua" and underneath, in a smaller font, "S.I.N.C. Active Resistance." In the photo, Teresa was smiling candidly at the camera; she was wearing jeans, an embroidered white blouse and had her hair tied in a ponytail. My sister was dressed in a tiny pair of red dungarees, her hair was in pigtails, and she wore an expression of extreme confusion. She was looking at Teresa rather than the camera. Behind them it was possible to make out the United States embassy on Paseo de la Reforma, and other demonstrators were advancing into frame on the right of the shot.

The second photograph was earlier than the first. It was smaller and the corners were rounded. In it, my father and Teresa stood with their arms around each other on a beach. My father's trunks were like a cropped, tight-fitting pair of boxers; he looked incredibly thin and had a ridiculous mustache. My mother's swimsuit hugged a six-months-pregnant belly. They were both smiling.

The third photograph was a family portrait, taken after my birth. Standing rather stiffly in front of the metal gate of the house in Educación, Teresa and my father were looking fixedly at the camera. At their feet was Mariana, wearing a flowered dress, and, almost wriggling from their arms, was a baby in floods of tears—me. I laughed a little on seeing that third image and decided to save it to give to Mariana, convinced that it would amuse her too.

The last photograph was a professional portrait of Teresa. The colors were more vivid than in the others, and it was a larger format. Standing alone, looking very serious, her face framed by those long bangs that were fashionable in the nineties, Teresa was looking at the camera with an aloof expression that communicated her disdain for the photographer, for the whole situation. The backdrop was of a blue fade that clashed with the red of her lipstick. Viewing that image, I thought that Teresa's makeup seemed overdone, as if she were disguising herself, as if that excess were a critique or parody. Her rigid, almost depressing seriousness reinforced that hypothesis and was slightly reminiscent of the expression in Buster Keaton's sad, wide-set eyes.

I put the photos to one side and continued to work through the folder. There were two electricity bills that seemed out of place there and, between them, an open envelope with postage stamps. I once again recognized Teresa's handwriting. The letter was addressed to my father and the return address was San Cristóbal de las Casas. From the date stamp I knew that my father must have read that letter, the second, shortly before Teresa's death.

Less passionate in tone than the first, the second letter was, by contrast, more informative. I guess that once she'd escaped, Teresa no longer felt the urgent need to justify herself ideologically, although her resolve was unshaken, perhaps even stronger than before. Without going into detail, she reproached my father for having made her abandon her interests, for having coaxed and wheedled her only then to reveal his true nature—a lack of moral principles, reactionary violence, rampant mediocrity. "Your money disgusts me," she said, "and because of you, I disgust myself."

After the paragraph of reproaches, Teresa went on to practical matters and the solid future she'd invented for herself. The future she'd perhaps spent years constructing or, on the other hand, had conceived in a moment of inspiration, crouched and vigilant in the Lacandon jungle.

She said that she'd moved to San Cristóbal de las Casas after attending the National Democratic Convention. Her plan was to get a job there and, at some point, bring Mariana to live with her. She promised to call us as soon as the telephone line was connected. She asked about my return to school, as if my father would reply to her letter—a letter that allowed for no possible answer, a letter that said everything there was to say between them. She sent me kisses.

I reread the letter a couple of times to make certain that I hadn't missed anything. I imagined my father rereading it, seething with rage, crumpling it in a moment of supreme frustration and then, early the following morning, repenting that action and smoothing it out again. Was that how it had been? Maybe not. Maybe my father had read it two or three times, put it in that red folder and forgotten about it. A few days afterward, Teresa had died and he hadn't given another thought to that letter; perhaps it had been easier, I thought, not to: easier to believe that his wife had died loving him unconditionally, promising to come home soon.

Setting aside what it meant for my father—and what it said about his ability to conceal the truth for years—the letter contained one eloquent and painful omission: Teresa had written that she would "bring Mariana" to live with her, and just that.

True, she did ask after me and sent me kisses, but there was no mention of bringing me to Chiapas.

What had Teresa seen in me that made her decide I wasn't worthy of that destiny? Did she think that I was too like my father, a violent man, without redeeming features, condemned to live in error, in mediocrity, in Educación?

I folded the letter along the existing crease and, as I did so, inevitably thought of the origami frog with the cryptic message ("the left side") I'd found in my bedroom. Folding folds, repeating the folds that others had made before me, seemed to be my fate. Teresa had folded that letter in September 1994. She'd put it in an envelope and walked to the post office in San Cristóbal de las Casas. Then, perhaps, she'd returned to the damp apartment with a metal door she'd rented in Santa Lucia or Barrio de Mexicanos, or wherever she'd decided to start her new life.

What had my mother done for the rest of that day? It's reasonable to suppose that she already had some friends: Zapatista sympathizers she'd met at the National Democratic Convention, indigenous women who had come from other parts of Mexico to learn from the rebels, local journalists who were accustomed to violence and death, and who both expected and feared betrayal by the government.

Sitting at my father's desk, the red folder open before me, I again felt like a detective, like the small, ten-year-old detective I'd wanted to be that summer. The same detective who had boarded a bus to nowhere, following a slender clue.

There were still a few documents in the folder that I hadn't looked at. One was my parents' marriage certificate, issued by Civil Register No. 49, Coyoacán, on April 4, 1978. Teresa's sprawling signature, my father's cramped, unclear signature, my grandparents' names. I put the dog-eared sheet of paper on top of a pile of important documents, next to the two letters.

The last document in the folder was Teresa's death certificate. I glanced over it distractedly, not intending to devote much time to it. I'd expected to find it in the desk. Just a little longer and I'd have completed my task: finished with that house, that story, that past. Rat and the refuse collector would, between them, remove the odds and ends left scattered about. I'd return to my shared apartment during the time it took Garmendia to sell the house and hand over my share of the inheritance. Now that I was unemployed, I'd have time to look for somewhere else to live. I'd choose one of the urban antipodes to Educación: an apartment in an interesting neighborhood with bookstores, and cafés that weren't El Jarocho. I'd look for a new job, or perhaps do a master's degree in something, now that I could afford to. And I didn't rule out the possibility of changing professions, or even moving to another city. I'd be able to travel abroad. All I had to do was fold that sheet of paper and it would be all over. The wide gash in the summer of '94 would close, would begin to heal.

I glanced down at the death certificate. The deceased's details. Name. Sex. The handwriting of the official who had filled in the form, his spelling mistakes. Spouse. Location: San Cristóbal de las Casas. Date of death: September 25, 1994. Not September 23. That's to say, the day after my father had flown to Chiapas. The day after, not the day before. Cause of death: Asphyxia due to inhalation of propane gas.

9

IT WAS A SLOW PROCESS. At first I behaved as if nothing had happened. After all, it could have been an error, there were a thousand explanations. I finished clearing out my father's house. I hired a van to transport the double bed and a few other things to my apartment. I called Garmendia and, two days later, gave him the keys to the house in Educación—all three extant sets.

One weekend I took a cab to my sister's, bringing with me the photographs I wanted to give her. Katia, her wife, laughed at the shots, but Mariana wasn't really amused. I also attempted to give her half the sum Rat had paid for the furniture, but she insisted I keep it: I'd need it more than she did now that I'd packed in my job.

In a matter of weeks, the house was sold: apparently Educación has become a trendy area, with most of the residents working in the business and retail zones of Coapa.

Throughout the following five months, I got on with my life as if nothing had happened. It could even be said that things improved, at least on the surface. I bought this apartment and moved in. Not having to pay rent was a great weight off my mind: I became a more cheerful person. I found a job in a company that produced educational diagnostic tests that was more lucrative than the Spanish classes. Each weekday morning, I put on a shirt I'd sent to be dry-cleaned and took the Metrobus to the modern building where I worked. I'd spend the day revising the grammar of questions for examinations in such diverse fields as mechatronic engineering and international law. The benefits were very good for such a simple task. I had paid vacation, health insurance, and a performance-related bonus if I checked more exam questions than my colleagues, which wasn't difficult because most people did very little work.

Mariana and I sometimes talked on the phone, and during the week we'd send text messages about trivia or to communicate the highlights of our daily lives.

During those months I also met a really nice woman, and we started dating. The fact that we worked near each other made it easier for us to meet. We went to the movie theater in the shopping mall or ate salads together at lunchtime. She was kind and seemed genuinely interested in me, an attitude I found—and still find—incomprehensible. She had a tinkling laugh, wide hips, and her left eye was slightly narrower than her right.

But I wasn't made for that life. It was as though I'd woken in someone else's body and was temporarily acting as a stand-in for that person.

I never mentioned the red folder to Mariana. I didn't tell her about the second letter or Teresa's plan to bring her to Chiapas to live with her. And of course, I didn't mention the death certificate, didn't mention the fissures that had opened up in the story my father had told us for years—the story we'd believed to be true, and from which our adult lives had ramified, like the veins from the midribs of my childhood leaves.

I kept the letter and the certificate in my own folder of important documents, which is green rather than red. A folder that I now keep under this bed, along with the elementary school notebooks and my passport.

I don't now remember what I was thinking about during those months. Nothing, I guess. I concentrated on functioning, on imagining a perfect future. My dry-cleaned shirts smelled the same as my father's used to, but I pretended not to notice.

One Sunday afternoon I took out the folder and contemplated it for a while. I extracted the contents and scattered the papers on top of my unmade bed. I didn't have the courage to read Teresa's letters again. The death certificate was folded in half, and I couldn't bring myself to open that either. I put everything back and returned the folder to its place under the bed.

That Sunday night I was unable to sleep. I wanted to force myself to cry, the way you make yourself vomit by sticking your fingers down your throat. I wanted my father to be alive so I could ask him what the hell had gone on in San Cristóbal de las Casas, in that small apartment where Teresa had chosen to remake her life. Ask him just exactly what had happened between September 23 and 25, 1994, while Mariana and I watched TV, while I vomited, had diarrhea, and drank cup after cup of chamomile tea, devastated by the news of Teresa's death.

But no one could respond to those questions then—no one can now. It's possible that the answer to them all has been forming in my subconscious during the past two years.

Maybe my father wanted me to find the answer alone, wanted the horror of that answer to grow inside me at its own pace, like a carnivorous plant that initially looks like clover and gradually reveals its true nature.

The following day I didn't go to the educational diagnostic test company. I was tired and upset, lacked the energy to continue pretending that everything was fine. The woman I was dating sent me four text messages, but I didn't reply to any of them. I convinced myself that I was ill, despite having no other symptom than a slight headache, probably due to a bad night's sleep.

On Tuesday, I returned to the office wearing my freshly laundered shirt. I found the Metrobus journey very difficult, but thought that once I got to work everything would be fine, that it was just a brief crisis. I told my boss that I was feeling better and said the usual good mornings to my colleagues. It occurred to me that I could perhaps make use of my untouched health insurance to consult a psychiatrist, a professional who would explain that what was happening to me was normal, a sort of delayed-action grief. I'd be prescribed something to help me sleep and that would be that.

But at one in the afternoon, just before the lunch break, I went to the restroom, shut the door, and stayed there for several minutes, feeling that I was about to scream or punch someone in the face. I left a message for my boss with his secretary and took a cab home. I never went back to that job. The people from human resources wrote repeatedly, asking what I wanted done with the things I'd left in my cubicle, but I never replied. I guess they must have thrown them out.

At first I used to go for short walks around the neighborhood, but as the days passed I spent increasing amounts of time in the apartment. I stopped taking showers, put on four or five pounds, began to order delivery meals—Hawaiian pizza. On Fridays, when Josefina came, I'd pretend to be working at the kitchen table so she wouldn't ask too many questions. But apart from those few hours, I was almost always in bed. Lying on the left side: Teresa's side.

After a couple of weeks, the woman I'd been dating began to show signs of annoyance. I told her I was ill, but when she offered to come by to see me, I stopped answering her messages. She continued calling but I didn't pick up. My ring tone was the chirping of crickets, so it didn't bother me.

One Saturday night she sent me a text saying that she was downstairs, at the entrance to the building. I let her in for fear she'd try to locate the caretaker or call the police. She was clearly concerned.

We had an awkward conversation, with her sitting on the edge of my bed, and me with the blankets pulled up to my chin. She asked if I still wanted to go on seeing her, I said I didn't, but I spoke the words very quietly and don't think she caught them; she asked me what I'd said. I didn't have the guts to repeat myself: I told her that I was going through a rough patch, but would be better soon and would get in touch then. Her tone was cold when she said good-bye (I don't blame her: I'd behaved like an asshole).

With Mariana, I managed to keep up the charade for longer. I used to answer her texts almost immediately; told her that I was happy with my new job and new girlfriend. In any case, she was always busy and rarely asked questions. But Josefina, who cleans Mariana's apartment on Tuesdays, told her that I was always at home, in pajamas, doing nothing. When my sister phoned to ask me about this, I invented a story, said that my hours had been cut and that I now had Fridays free, but something in her voice gave me the impression that she didn't believe me. A few days afterward, I told her I'd been fired. She asked if I was looking for work and my reply was, "not for the time being," putting an end to the issue.

For the most part of the last two years, my life has been confined to this bed. I sometimes sit up, resting my back against the wall, and look through the window at the only view: the office building across the street.

In the beginning I used to think about Teresa a lot: I was trying to recall as clearly as possible the unvarying tone of her voice, the color of her hair, the way she smoked, leaning against the wall of the house in Educación. But the truth is that I only lived with Teresa during the first ten years of my life, so I don't have many memories of her. I've set down here the three or four that are clearest (Teresa fainting on the edge of the market, Teresa walking behind me as I chased pigeons, Teresa arguing with my father, Teresa going camping one Tuesday at midday) in order to fix them in some way, to see if my memory finally stops distorting them, and the replica of the replica of the replica halts its slow but certain decay.

The image of my father, by contrast, has more points of reference: two more decades of meetings, silences, and meals eaten together. The memory of him in 1994 is frequently superimposed by the memory of my ailing father, sedated in his hospital bed, a morphine-induced smile on his face. I occasionally manage to forget that he's dead, and I imagine him sitting in an armchair in the living room, shouting at a rerun of a soccer game. In my imagination, I'm sitting beside him, but instead of looking at the TV set, I'm carefully observing each of his features—searching for myself in them, terrified by the acceptance that they are also mine.

One part of me knows that I can't stay in this bed forever. Lately I've been thinking of making drastic changes. Perhaps I'll go to San Cristóbal de las Casas. Or better still, I'll take a bus to Villahermosa, where I can start a new life, with another name (Úlrich González, for example). The new life of someone who had no father, no mother, who didn't kick a pigeon in a square in Mexico City or lose anything in September 1994.

Perhaps, before boarding the bus, I'll take a walk through the area around the Taxqueña terminal, the streets of Colonia Educación, attempting to understand the nuances of the unspeakable answer that has been growing inside me, devouring me. Perhaps, before changing my name, I'll also walk to the cemetery where I buried my father, to scream at him in a way I was never capable of screaming when he was alive—the way my sister and my mother used to scream at him when he was still a part of their lives. But before doing anything, before thinking about getting out of bed, before finally becoming the person I always should have been, I'd like to finish writing this.

ACKNOWLEDGMENTS

The author would like to thank the Mexican Fondo Nacional para la Cultura y las Artes (FONCA) and the Banff Centre for Arts and Creativity for their support in the writing of this book.

Coffee House Press began as a small letterpress operation in 1972 and has grown into an internationally renowned nonprofit publisher of literary fiction, essay, poetry, and other work that doesn't fit neatly into genre categories.

Coffee House is both a publisher and an arts organization. Through our *Books in Action* program and publications, we've become interdisciplinary collaborators and incubators for new work and audience experiences. Our vision for the future is one where a publisher is a catalyst and connector.

LITERATURE
is not the same thing as
PUBLISHING

Funder Acknowledgments

Coffee House Press is an internationally renowned independent book publisher and arts nonprofit based in Minneapolis, MN; through its literary publications and *Books in Action* program, Coffee House acts as a catalyst and connector—between authors and readers, ideas and resources, creativity and community, inspiration and action.

Coffee House Press books are made possible through the generous support of grants and donations from corporations, state and federal grant programs, family foundations, and the many individuals who believe in the transformational power of literature. This activity is made possible by the voters of Minnesota through a Minnesota State Arts Board Operating Support grant, thanks to the legislative appropriation from the Arts and Cultural Heritage Fund. Coffee House also receives major operating support from the Amazon Literary Partnership, Jerome Foundation, McKnight Foundation, Target Foundation, and the National Endowment for the Arts (NEA). To find out more about how NEA grants impact individuals and communities, visit www.arts.gov.

Coffee House Press receives additional support from the Elmer L. & Eleanor J. Andersen Foundation; the David & Mary Anderson Family Foundation; Bookmobile; Dorsey & Whitney LLP; Foundation Technologies; Fredrikson & Byron, P.A.; the Fringe Foundation; Kenneth Koch Literary Estate; the Matching Grant Program Fund of the Minneapolis Foundation; Mr. Pancks' Fund in memory of Graham Kimpton; the Schwab Charitable Fund; Schwegman, Lundberg & Woessner, P.A.; the Silicon Valley Community Foundation; and the U.S. Bank Foundation.

The Publisher's Circle of Coffee House Press

Publisher's Circle members make significant contributions to Coffee House Press's annual giving campaign. Understanding that a strong financial base is necessary for the press to meet the challenges and opportunities that arise each year, this group plays a crucial part in the success of Coffee House's mission.

Recent Publisher's Circle members include many anonymous donors, Patricia A. Beithon, the E. Thomas Binger & Rebecca Rand Fund of the Minneapolis Foundation, Andrew Brantingham, Dave & Kelli Cloutier, Louise Copeland, Jane Dalrymple-Hollo & Stephen Parlato, Mary Ebert & Paul Stembler, Kaywin Feldman & Jim Lutz, Chris Fischbach & Katie Dublinski, Sally French, Jocelyn Hale & Glenn Miller, the Rehael Fund-Roger Hale/Nor Hall of the Minneapolis Foundation, Randy Hartten & Ron Lotz, Dylan Hicks & Nina Hale, William Hardacker, Randall Heath, Jeffrey Hom, Carl & Heidi Horsch, the Amy L. Hubbard & Geoffrey J. Kehoe Fund, Kenneth & Susan Kahn, Stephen & Isabel Keating, Julia Klein, the Kenneth Koch Literary Estate, Cinda Kornblum, Jennifer Kwon Dobbs & Stefan Liess, the Lambert Family Foundation, the Lenfestey Family Foundation, Joy Linsday Crow, Sarah Lutman & Rob Rudolph, the Carol & Aaron Mack Charitable Fund of the Minneapolis Foundation, George & Olga Mack, Joshua Mack & Ron Warren, Gillian McCain, Malcolm S. McDermid & Katie Windle, Mary & Malcolm McDermid, Sjur Midness & Briar Andresen, Daniel N. Smith III & Maureen Millea Smith, Peter Nelson & Jennifer Swenson, Enrique & Jennifer Olivarez, Alan Polsky, Robin Preble, Alexis Scott, Ruth Stricker Dayton, Jeffrey Sugerman & Sarah Schultz, Nan G. Swid, Kenneth Thorp in memory of Allan Kornblum & Rochelle Ratner, Patricia Tilton, Stu Wilson & Melissa Barker, Warren D. Woessner & Iris C. Freeman, and Margaret Wurtele.

For more information about the Publisher's Circle and other ways to support Coffee House Press books, authors, and activities, please visit www.coffeehousepress.org/pages/donate or contact us at info@coffeehousepress.org.

Daniel Saldaña París is an essayist, poet, and novelist born in Mexico City. His debut novel, *Among Strange Victims,* was a finalist for the 2017 Best Translated Book Award. His work has appeared in *BOMB, Guernica, Literary Hub, Electric Literature,* the *Guardian,* and elsewhere. In 2017, he was named by the Hay Festival as one of the best Latin American writers under the age of forty.

Christina MacSweeney was awarded the 2016 Valle Inclán Translation Prize for her translation of Valeria Luiselli's *The Story of My Teeth,* and her translation of Daniel Saldaña París's novel *Among Strange Victims* was a finalist for the 2017 Best Translated Book Award. She works regularly with authors such as Elvira Navarro, Verónica Gerber Bicecci, and Julián Herbert.

Ramifications was designed by
Bookmobile Design & Digital Publisher Services.
Text is set in Minion Pro.